"Get away w

Zachary warned.

"*Excuse me?*" Stunned, Willa couldn't have budged now if she wanted to.

"You heard me. It's dangerous for someone like you."

"Someone like me? You're going to have to spell that one out," she said, growing more angry every second. "Exactly what are you driving at?"

He nodded as though she'd satisfied some private question. "Yes, you look like a woman who wants to hear men say it. Beautiful. And alone."

A surprisingly cool breeze blew in through the screen door, and Willa shivered. It felt like phantom hands stroking her arms.

"But I'm hardly alone, am I, Mr. Denton? After all, I have you to watch over me."

Something mesmerizing and yet untamed flared in his eyes. "That's your biggest danger."

Helen R. Myers satisfies her preference for a reclusive lifestyle by living deep in the Piney Woods of east Texas with her husband, Robert, and—because they were there first—the various species of four-legged and winged creatures that wander throughout their ranch. To write has been her lifelong dream, and to bring a slightly different flavor to each book is an ongoing ambition.

Admittedly restless, she feels this trait helps her writing. "It makes me reach for new territory and experiment with old boundaries." In 1993 the Romance Writers of America awarded *Navarrone* the prestigious RITA Award for Best Short Contemporary Novel of the Year.

WATCHING FOR WILLA

HELEN R. MYERS

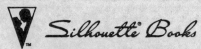

Published by Silhouette Books

America's Publisher of Contemporary Romance

SILHOUETTE BOOKS

ISBN 0-373-51186-8

WATCHING FOR WILLA

This edition published by arrangement with Harlequin Books S.A.

® and TM are trademarks of Harlequin Books S.A., used under license. Trademarks indicated with ® are registered in the United States Patent and Trademark Office, the Canadian Trade Marks Office and in other countries.

Visit Silhouette at www.eHarlequin.com

Printed in U.S.A.

CHAPTER ONE

He sat motionless behind the faded blue net drapes and watched his new neighbor dash from the house to the van for another box. Thunder rumbled endlessly, as only spring thunder could, underscoring the assault of rain as it machine-gunned the gutters. The combination of sounds sent something rattling precariously behind him. The racket compounded an already brutal three-aspirin headache; still, he took considerable pleasure in seeing the woman getting drenched. She deserved to be miserable, and he hoped each trip from van to house added to her disgust. It would serve her right for buying the vacant Miller place. Little fool...she wasn't asking for trouble, she was provoking it.

It had been her arrival, the slam of the driver's door that had roused him from yet another drunken nap. His third...or was it the fourth of the morning? It didn't surprise him that he'd lost count of how often he'd drifted in and out of consciousness; when he worked himself to the point of exhaustion, he could sleep through a tornado. Once he'd done just that. But the sound of another human presence always put him on the alert. Ignoring the need to brush the foul taste of Scotch from his mouth, to shower and get a potful of coffee into his system, he gripped the chair's padded arms and leaned forward to peer outside, keenly aware that the time he'd been dreading had come. Actually, he'd been waiting for it, aware of its inevitability ever since the For Sale sign disappeared from the front of the empty two-story house. And now he had another reason to dread the event because everything about her was right, which made her wrong, *dead* wrong to be here.

As he exhaled, the sheers shifted subtly, his vision blurred and a wave of nausea swept through him. Those reactions, however, had less to do with his hangover than with fury. He knew what this intrusion meant, what she was forcing him to do, and he resented her for putting him in this predicament. But heaven help him, she was something to look at…as perfect and stunning a target as those first teasing glimpses of her had led him to believe.

Fair and shapely, she was a shimmering woman who became more so courtesy of the rain drenching her and plastering her tank top and leggings to her body. The fact that both were white, and that she wasn't wearing a bra fueled his imagination, and forced him to remember cravings he preferred to forget, and anticipate horrors that might be even too terrible for one of his books.

Despite the distance and the downpour, he could see the full delineation of her breasts, the tautness of her nipples. He could also see that she wore bikini briefs beneath her leggings. Not much of a pair, he thought, his mouth going dry as she stretched to reach for something from deep inside the van.

Out came a plastic pail loaded with what he figured were cleaning products, followed by a mop. The head of the mop got stuck on something and she had to jerk it free. That sent her ponytail swinging across her shoulders; several shades of blond, it made him wonder about the color of her eyes. When he'd first seen her, he'd guessed aquamarine blue, pale and aloof like the business suit she'd been wearing. Now he wondered if they weren't the vibrant green of the lush shrubbery she momentarily disappeared behind. By the time she reappeared, hurrying along the sidewalk and up the stone steps to the porch, he decided that whatever color they were, she looked and moved like money. Some women were gifted that way, born with an indefinable quality, an aura of elegance, even when dressed in something someone else might use as a polishing cloth.

All the more reason to resent her arrival.

What had possessed her to move into that relic next door? The question so agitated him that he wanted to rip down the drapes and shout at her through the screen. The old-fashioned house was all wrong, totally out of character for someone like her—and didn't she read the papers? Listen to rumors? Was she that naive to think living away from town, down a dead-end street, would protect her from what was going on? She must be, otherwise she would have realized how, instead, she'd placed herself in the path of danger. No, directly at hell's doorway.

Her laugh, spontaneous and breathless as she dropped everything and shook rain from her hair, cut off his brooding and had him shifting to peer through the slight part between the draperies. He wasn't used to laughter, at least not this lighthearted and happy. What had elicited it? he wondered, frowning because it made no sense. The weather was lousy, the house a white elephant.... He'd overestimated her, all right. The woman wasn't merely guilty of bad judgment, she was a fool with the survival instincts of a moth.

Once again he glared at her new home. Some investment. It couldn't be considered a smart one under any circumstances. Over fifty years old, the place was what people in the real estate business generously called "quaint," a "fixer-upper." *He* saw it as approximately eighteen-hundred square feet of stone-encased trouble. Granted, the roof had been reshingled, and the foundation cracks repaired—he'd been forced to suffer through the interminable racket and could bear witness to a job well-done—but considering how long it had remained empty, he had a hunch a great deal more needed attention.

A woman all alone in the world had to be nuts to take on such responsibility. As he thought of her marital status, which he'd first suspected and later confirmed, a pain seared through his head—but most unwelcome was the surge of heat that shot into his loins.

Alone...alone...alone.

Yes, that was the ultimate temptation.

It was a relief when she unlocked the front door and disappeared inside. Slumping back in his chair, he waited for the tension inside him to ease. It took its damned time. Long enough for a seed of an idea to germinate in the barren wilderness that was his mind these days. Grow...and...expand, until he forgot about the craving for coffee. "My God. *Yes!*"

With the grit of sleep and the sting of too many wasted hours at the computer burning his eyes, he spun around his wheelchair to face the computer monitor's blue screen and began typing with feverish zeal.

Despite the several thousand dollars she'd already invested, the inside of the house still resembled a nightmare: scratched and dirty walls, filthy hardwood floors, cracked or missing chandeliers, and more. But she loved the place because it was now officially *her* nightmare. Besides, she'd always had an imagination to match her energy; she could handle this.

Glancing around with more optimism than intimidation, she knew that given a few days, she would perform miracles. It wasn't only the feminine form that she had a talent for enhancing.

Pushing the pail of cleaning supplies farther into the small entryway, she elbowed the door shut behind her, and once again wiped at the rain streaking down her face. "Well, Willa," she drawled to the room at large, "you've taken on a handful now."

Back when she'd first opened Whimsy by Willa in downtown Vilary, her family, as well as legal and accounting advisers, had insisted that a woman's intimate apparel shop could never survive in the county seat's town square, even though many of the community's residents were upscale commuters who worked in Houston. Yuppies or no yuppies, economic recovery, or outright boomtown, they'd argued, Vilary remained staunchly conservative. She would lose the insurance money she'd received after A.J.'s death, maybe end up having to file for bankruptcy.

Eleven months later, when she'd moved the increasingly popular boutique to its larger facilities at the new mall on the fringes of town, the lecturing started all over again. But this time she hadn't bothered pretending to listen. She'd known that taking the slot next to the Vilary Vantage Health Club and Spa was financially a wise move, despite the intimidating rent. And now, six months later, she was proving herself right.

She planned on being as on target about her new home, too, regardless of everyone else's pessimism. Yes, the place would need a great deal of her attention, but the condition of the house was primarily a result of neglect, and the minor vandalism that had occurred was thoroughly understandable. The old woman who'd owned it had spent her last years in a nursing home, and her children had lived out of state. It had been impossible to watch over the house as closely as anyone would have liked.

Willa didn't intend to be swayed or frightened by the criticism over her new home's isolated location, either. Who cared if there was only one other house at this end of the dead-end street and that except for it she was surrounded by woods? That just made the setting more appealing to her.

After spending so much of her day dealing with employees, customers and suppliers, she'd been yearning to move from her rented duplex, to find someplace where she could relax, and rejuvenate both her energy level and her creativity. This secluded property promised to give her that, and she refused to feel threatened because of the unfortunate stalkings going on in the area. Yes, like every other woman in town, she was taking precautions. She double-checked all doors and windows, carried tear gas, tried to be observant and aware of what was going on around her.

But the police were doing their part, too. They had increased and intensified their presence in the community, and in their last statement they'd sounded reassured that perhaps the stalker had left the area. At least there hadn't been any report of him since the third incident almost ten days ago.

At any rate, she wasn't alone, not really. Thinking of the house that stood only a few dozen yards from her own, she went to the double window in the small dining room and considered the two-story, vintage Victorian.

Willa shook her head. Her accountant had dubbed her place "The Eyesore," but *that* monstrosity was nearly as spooky as its celebrated occupant—and ugly enough to scare off the dead, let alone some demented soul bent on terrifying women.

But neglected mess or not, she still couldn't believe it. She, Willa Leeds Whitney, was living next door to Zachary Denton, the most successful horror writer since Stephen King! Mr. Denton, however, was the true recluse, and for good reason.

He was confined to a wheelchair, the result of a flying accident three years ago. Although news about the crash had received media-wide coverage, her real-estate agent had been eager to repeat everything *she'd* ever heard about the incident. Willa had changed the subject as soon as possible, though, not wanting to seem like a snoop, or to be reminded of her own loss. Plus, she figured that if she was meant to know anything else, fate would see she found out soon enough. Who knows? Zachary Denton might tell her himself. Then again, probably not. Mrs. Landers did mention he was worse than ever these days, a certified misanthrope. Willa certainly wasn't about to begrudge him his right to privacy. She did, however, hope he appreciated having survived the crash. Her A.J. hadn't been so lucky.

Did Zachary Denton know the house had been sold? Did he care? Well, he needn't have any concerns that she would bother him. As she noted each successive window, how all the drapes or shutters were tightly shut, she thought he might find it reassuring to understand that she valued her privacy, too. True, the consensus that she never met a stranger was accurate—she liked people and found it easy to strike up conversations with just about anyone—but no one had ever called her a star-struck groupie. Nor was she the stereotypical lonely widow. After what she and A.J. had shared in their all-too-brief time together, she would never settle for anything less; and since that wasn't likely to happen, she was content to live her life alone and expend her considerable energy toward other interests.

Her gaze settled on the top floor of her neighbor's house, specifically the window directly opposite the bedroom she'd chosen for herself. Unlike the other windows, it was open to the rain, and the mild breeze gently billowed the sheers. Was that a TV beyond them? No...a computer screen.

Could that be his office where he conjured all those twisted stories? Fascinating. But she shivered, too.

It was from being wet and chilled, she told herself, not because of his dark imaginings. A self-deprecating smile tugged at the left corner of her mouth. Goodness, she hadn't had one of his books around since... The smile withered, and she wondered how she could have forgotten. It had been the night she'd awakened to the sound of the ringing telephone, reached across A.J.'s copy of *The Well*, only to learn that her husband's emergency medical helicopter had gone down in a storm.

Willa backed away from the window and rubbed her bare arms. "All right, you had your ten seconds of self-pity, now stop it."

She had too much work ahead of her to succumb to melancholia. It was Friday and, ready or not, on Monday morning the movers would be transferring her things here from her apartment across town. Even then there would be plenty of projects left to fill a month of weekends, let alone this one. Floors needed to be scrubbed, wallpaper had to be wiped down, and a mile of trim needed to be painted; but before she started any of that she had the kitchen and bathrooms to scour.

For a moment she wondered if she hadn't been a bit obstinate in insisting on handling everything herself.

Then she shook her head and went to get her cleaning supplies. Of course, she could handle this; she had pep and determination to spare. Besides, there wasn't anyone available to help even if she had wanted it. Her staff at Whimsy was busy with the store's big spring sale, her parents were on their annual vacation—this time touring Europe—and in a few weeks her sister was going to make her an aunt for the second time. No way would Willa let her drive down from Dallas, let alone consider seeing her overexert herself doing housework. The only option if she couldn't "solo" this job was to contract help, and that was—

"Oh, no."

She'd carried the pail, mop and cleaning supplies to the kitchen, and had turned on the water taps, only to find nothing came out. This couldn't be happening to her! Yesterday, the city water department had guaranteed she would have service by that afternoon!

She glanced at her watch. It was almost nine. Someone down there had to be in the office by now, but she had no telephone service yet, and wouldn't until later today. That's *if* the telephone company proved more reliable than the water people.

What to do...?

She could drive back to town and handle things in person, but she was hardly dressed for taking care of that kind of business, even if she slipped on the oversize shirt she'd left in the van. She could go back to the duplex and call from there, except that it was even farther out of town. It would be such a waste to lose that much time.

Biting her lower lip, she once again looked out the window at the gloomy house only a few dozen yards away. Would Zachary Denton let her use his telephone?

From what she'd heard about his zealous protection of
his privacy, she doubted it. On the other hand, who
would turn away a neighbor in need?

She had nothing to lose by asking.

CHAPTER TWO

The downpour hadn't eased a bit. Once outside, Willa sprinted across the two overgrown yards trying not to think about snakes and any other crawling creature. What with the lightning getting closer, she told herself she probably had more to fear from it. Concentrating on her neighbor's home helped, too.

Zachary Denton's house belonged in one of his books. Not only did it need a new coat or two of paint—and in a color less morbid than the current grim brown—the junipers and Chinese loquats surrounding it had grown past several of the first-floor windows adding to the general aura of wild neglect. As she dashed up the cracked sidewalk, Willa reasoned maintenance would be difficult, if not impossible, for someone who'd been incapacitated. But the man could easily afford to hire someone, several someones, to periodically clean up around here.

Sprinting up the creaking ramp instead of the stairs, she hurried across the wooden porch to search for a doorbell. As far as she could tell there wasn't any. Ridiculous, she fumed, feeling like a half-drowned rat. About to knock on the outer screen door, she spotted the security camera out of the corner of her left eye.

Was it running? A momentary spasm of self-consciousness had her wanting to turn her back to it, to dash for the haven of her own four walls. Although she hated to waste time bemoaning hindsight, she also wished she'd taken a second to retrieve that damned shirt. But a sudden, close flash of lightning followed by an ominous crash of thunder stopped that wistful thought.

Get it over with, she told herself. The sooner she made the call, the faster her problem would be solved. Anyway, a man in his condition wasn't likely to pay attention to her in *that* way, was he?

Frowning, she knocked briskly, and waited.

Since his computer monitor was on, that probably meant he was awake and working. How long should it take him to get down here? How would he manage? She crossed her arms again regretting her state of dress. But, no, she'd wanted comfort because of the humidity and the dirty job ahead of her.

She knocked again. "Excuse me! Anyone home? I need help!"

Several more seconds passed. She leaned closer to the door to listen, but as far as she could tell it was as quiet as a mausoleum in there.

Surely he wouldn't ignore her? Had he suffered a hearing problem along with his other injuries?

Just when she was about to knock more forcefully, she heard a click and then the hardwood door swung open. The long accompanying creak had the hairs on Willa's arms and at the back of her neck rising. But it wasn't only the eerie sound that got to her, it was the realization that no one was there!

Don't you dare start again. As dark as it was in there, she just hadn't seen him yet, that was all.

Holding fast to that logic, she cupped her hands around her eyes and peered through the screen. Seeing the cavernous foyer, she decided to try the handle of the outer door. To her surprise it was unlatched.

She opened it slightly and stepped inside. *Careful.*

She glanced around the hardwood door. Even if her neighbor was a bestselling writer, it would be foolish to take anything for granted. Anyone could get a little crazy if they found a stranger in their home; what's more, hadn't she read that after the crash, Zachary Denton had been accused by his own wife of becoming "twisted"? Anyway, Willa supposed a person had to be a bit strange to create such convoluted stories as he did.

But instead of discovering someone hiding behind the door, she found a metal armlike mechanism attached to a motor box that was bolted to the inside of the door. Well, well, she mused. So that's how he did it. Clever contraption.

"What kind of help?"

The unexpected demand almost made her yelp like one of the high school girls who worked at her store on weekends. But as she spun around, she decided it was a good thing she continued to hold on to the door; it helped her stand her ground, rather than run.

He sat on his wheeled throne at the top of the stairs, and although it was quite dark, one glance and the impulse to offer a bright, friendly smile evaporated. In its place emerged renewed doubt, and growing trepidation.

This was Zachary Denton? She swallowed, but her heart stayed stubbornly locked in her throat. Whatever she'd been expecting, it wasn't this cross between a grizzly bear and a wild man.

The only picture she'd ever seen of him was the one on the back of his books. In it, he'd been posed leaning against a single-engine plane, the same one he'd ridden to the ground shortly after takeoff at Houston's Hobby Airport. The black-and-white photograph had captured a man no more than thirty, tall and physically fit, but

hardly muscle-bound; and although attractive, even intense, he'd hardly looked the sort to spend so much time
focused on the dark side of human nature. The man
glaring down at her was a different story entirely.

The fierce-eyed, scraggly bearded sentinel above had
the haunted face of someone who could be at least a
decade older—until you looked at the rest of him. Even
from down here, she could tell he wasn't anything close
to the atrophied wreck she'd expected. Within what
looked like a moth-eaten sleeveless sweatshirt was a
body that seemed capable of bench pressing someone
twice his size. It made her grateful for the distance between them.

"I asked you a question. What kind of help?"

His sharp reprimand snapped her out of her trance.
"Excuse me. I'm—"

"I know who you are."

He did? Had he seen her pull in next door? She
wanted to ask, but his stare stopped her. It wasn't that
being looked at was a new experience for her; she and
Kelly had been blessed with good genes, inheriting the
best features from their striking parents, and as a result
had always attracted their share of attention. But few
people tended to be quite this…direct about it. Zachary
Denton's visual inventory felt anything but flattering; it
was almost an assault!

"I don't like people wandering around out there."
His voice echoed off the high ceiling and dark-paneled
walls, sounding not too different than the rumbling
thunder. "When they do, I find out why."

The accusation gave her the courage to reply. "Then
you know I'm not wandering. I'm your new neighbor."
She pointed behind her with her thumb. "11 Raven
Lane?"

When she'd first read the street sign down the block, she'd chuckled, reminded of Poe's famous poem. Now she wondered if the road hadn't been named *after* Zachary Denton moved in.

"Well, this isn't 11, it's 13, so what do you want?"

What a charmer. Bet anything his house suffered a good trashing from disappointed kids on Halloween, she thought with disappointment. For A.J., of course; how crushed her husband would have been if he'd discovered his favorite writer was a big…creep. Maybe the man had suffered a horrible tragedy, but he wasn't the first to do so. A person needed to pull himself together and get on with life. All Zachary Denton seemed to have done was entomb himself.

On the other hand, she wasn't about to offend the man. She needed his help too much to risk getting thrown out.

Moistening her lips, she tried to ignore the deep shadows filling every corner, or how angry the rain sounded beating against his house. "Mr. Denton, if you'll just let me borrow your telephone, I'll be on my way in a minute. You see, I was told the water would be on at my place, but apparently someone didn't make it out here yesterday."

"No, they didn't."

So he didn't miss anything from his second floor observation point. Wouldn't George Orwell have found this "Big Brother" inspiring?

When he didn't add anything else, Willa sighed inwardly and continued. "Yes, well, unfortunately, my telephone isn't hooked up yet—I mean, either." Good grief, the man was turning her into a babbling ninny.

"Only a fool would be alone over there without a phone."

She couldn't believe his gall! That did it; as soon as she moved in, she intended to lease one of those cellular models. No way did she intend to deal with this caustic, ungenerous...*writer* again! "That matter should be taken care of shortly," she assured him, holding fast to the last shreds of her manners, if not her goodwill. "In a few hours at the most."

"Yes...but sometimes a few hours can feel like an eternity."

It was a warning despite the softer delivery. It sent another chill racing through her, and she wrapped her arms around herself, barely managing to resist rubbing them again. How dare he entertain himself by attempting to unnerve her! Worse, he'd succeeded. And it wasn't merely the threat she had a sudden urge to run from, it was an inescapable something reaching for her through his dark, hypnotic stare...something blatant and physical. Something...sexual?

Are you crazy? The man's in a wheelchair for pity's sake!

Willa straightened and tried to look like the businesswoman she was, polite but cool. Clearly, she'd made a mistake. He'd gotten the wrong impression from the way she was dressed. It was too late to do anything about that; however, she intended to let him know she didn't unravel quite as easily as he seemed to want.

"I'll be fine, Mr. Denton, but thank you for your concern." Trying not to appear anxious as she glanced around, she spotted the phone on the side table not three yards away. "Oh, I see it right here. If you don't mind, I'll—"

"If you have any sense, you won't move into that house. Get away while you can."

"Excuse me?" Stunned, she couldn't have budged now if she wanted to.

"You heard me. It's all wrong...dangerous for someone like you."

"Someone like me? That one you're going to have to spell out," she said growing more angry with every second. "Exactly what are you driving at?"

He nodded as though she'd satisfied some private question. "Yes, you look like a woman who wants to hear men say it. Beautiful."

"That's not what I meant," she snapped with a dismissing wave.

"And alone."

A surprisingly cool breeze blew in through the screen door and Willa shivered. It was because it felt like phantom hands stroking her arms, she insisted to herself as goose bumps sprang up on her skin. She wouldn't let it be *him.* He was just playing games to scare her, toying with her mind to make sure she never bothered him again.

Fury gave her the nerve to shift her hands to her hips and take a few steps toward him. It brought her directly under the single, but dim chandelier light. She wanted to make sure he had an excellent view; then she gave him the slow smile that used to make A.J. start breathing like a freight train engine carrying one car too many. "But I'm hardly alone am I, Mr. Denton? After all, I have you to watch over me."

Something mesmerizing and yet untamed flared in his eyes. "That's your biggest danger." This time he was the one to point to the phone. "Make your call. You have three minutes before I reset the electronic bolt lock. You don't want to be on the wrong side of that door when I do."

Willa stared, speechless, until he disappeared into a room and slammed the door behind him. Surely he didn't mean that?

But what if he did?

Most important, what was that nonsense about his being dangerous to her? She didn't care for that threat one bit, or how it reminded her of the stalkings going on around Vilary.

Get a grip, kiddo. The only thing she could take comfort in was knowing that a man in Zachary Denton's condition was about as likely to be connected with the trouble in town as it was apt to snow tonight.

Wishing she'd never come over here, Willa hurried across the room and snatched up the telephone's receiver. Only then did she notice that her hand was shaking. Zachary Denton had achieved what he'd set out to do: he'd frightened her. In fact he'd left her trembling all over.

He waited until late to make his move, waited until she'd returned from another trip to town and had shut off the lights for the night. He'd begun to think she never would. What an energetic one, he thought, circling the house to peer in the uncurtained windows to make sure she had given up the scrubbing and polishing for the day.

Determined, too. She had to be to spend the night in a sleeping bag on the floor. He'd seen her retrieve the thing from the van a short while ago. He would have to remember that about her. It meant she wouldn't be a pushover; not at all like the others, who'd proved no challenge, making him lose interest.

He'd already discovered much from simply watching her. Yes, she was the best so far. The least like Judith, though, except for the hair…and the eyes. But that was okay. What was important was that she was here, conveniently within reach.

The sudden flash of the overhead light in her kitchen made him recoil and press flat back against the cool damp stones of the house. Damn, now what? His heart pounded surging adrenaline through him like a pulsating sprinkler system gone haywire. Had she spotted him? He hadn't heard a scream. But what if she'd run to the phone to call the police? He had to check and find out.

Easing to the window again, he peered around the metal trim. No, he'd let himself worry for nothing. Apparently, she was only thirsty and had come down to get a drink. He watched her fill a glass with ice cubes, then bottled water from the refrigerator.

His confidence returned and with it came lust. But all too soon he had to press himself back against the unyielding stone because her skimpy top and panties left little to the imagination.

He wanted to touch her breasts. He rubbed his hands over smooth mortar and stone pretending it was her flesh. He wanted to hurt her, knowing she would be aroused; he wanted to hear her beg him to stop, though he knew she wouldn't really mean it.

He owed Judith for teaching him that secret. If not for her, he might never have discovered his hidden talent, his great power. And soon beautiful Willa would know it, too…would know his power.

He imagined the ecstasy that moment would bring, the feel of his hands around her creamy throat as she drew him deeper and deeper inside her body. That would be the best moment because the harder he squeezed, the sooner her face would become Judith's…desirable, untouchable…cruel, untouchable Judith. Only then would he let the fiery red sea of excitement and pleasure consume him.

If only he could tell Willa now how fantastic it was going to be. But it was too soon. "Much too soon," he groaned in misery as he rocked his feverish forehead against the night-cooled stone. His pelvis, too.

Then he stopped. Another idea was forming.

If he hurried, he could do something. He could be her first thought in the morning. It wasn't enough, not nearly, he thought as the house went dark again, but it was a beginning.

Eager to get started, he stumbled off into the night.

CHAPTER THREE

She stretched, as far as the sleeping bag allowed, and took her time before opening her eyes. Waking had always been a sensual experience to her, much like indulging in a long bubble bath, slipping into something sleek and silky or making love. Something to be enjoyed thoroughly or not at all. Her mattress hadn't been ideal—now thirty, she had to admit she preferred the comforts of a conventional bed to roughing it with the equipment she and A.J. had used back when they'd been hikers and campers—but there was nothing like the sleep that followed a day of all-out physical labor to make a hard floor inconsequential.

Ready for some coffee and round two, she finally flipped back the top of her unzipped sleeping bag and rolled herself up onto her feet. She stretched again as she padded to the bathroom. By the light already spilling in through the windows she estimated it was around six o'clock, her favorite hour to start the day. All she needed now was coffee and a banana, her breakfast almost every morning. After that she would be ready to start painting.

When she came out of the bathroom, still toweling her face dry, she thought about the newspaper and hoped she would find one on her driveway when she got downstairs. Thank goodness the paperboy had been running late yesterday; she'd intercepted him and he'd agreed to add her to his route starting today. She liked to ease into her mornings with the paper. Not via the front pages, though. After A.J. died, she'd stopped giving herself an ulcer over what they printed *there*.

What appealed to her was browsing through the home and living sections, the fashions and finally the comics. Who cared if her accountant brother-in-law rolled his eyes at that? Willa smiled as she hung up the single bath towel she'd brought from the duplex. Jack could chide and lecture all he wanted about how a businesswoman needed to pay attention to the financial news. As far as she was concerned, her "business" was understanding women and their fantasies. Nothing she'd ever read in the so-called serious sections of the paper had ever helped her or anyone she knew have a happier more satisfying relationship with a lover or spouse. In fact, from her vantage point, those killed romance.

An article about how more people were adding fountains into their homes for their ornateness as well as their soothing effect, inspired her to invest in one for the entryway of her store. As anticipated, it soon lured passers-by, who then became intrigued with the sensual massage and bath products she displayed around the fountain.

And that hadn't been an isolated experiment. The fashion sections of the paper helped her determine upcoming color trends and styles for her lingerie and loungewear inventory. The comics gave her a lift on days when being an entrepreneur seemed to be the most insane choice a woman in her situation could make. Let the financial moguls posture and pontificate on the business section's pages; she'd never met one who understood how to tell his slightly plump wife that he would love to see her in a sexy item of lingerie or robe.

Willa bent at the waist and brushed her long hair forward from the nape. Thinking of robes reminded her that she needed to call Starla and remind her about the short silk ones they were going to bring out of stock to add to the sale merchandise today. Then again, maybe she shouldn't. Her young assistant manager would utter a funny, theatrical groan, but underneath would be a subtle accusation about not being trusted. Willa knew she'd already pushed her luck. Yesterday she'd dialed to pass on her new number, then she'd phoned to check how sales were going. And she'd called again later that night to make sure Starla remembered to lock up securely.

No, she wouldn't do it. Everything was under control. If she felt like a mother away from her baby for the first time, that was her problem, one she'd better keep to herself—unless she wanted to risk losing a valuable employee, as well as someone she'd come to care for as a friend.

Straightening and flinging her hair back over her shoulders, her gaze settled on the windows of her bedroom...and beyond. To his house. *Those* windows.

Her heart gave a jolt as she saw the dark silhouette behind the net draperies. It was him. For a few blissful moments she'd actually managed to push yesterday's disturbing incident to the back of her mind, and now the man had the gall to be spying on her like some... Peeping Tom!

She felt the strongest urge to hide behind the bathroom door, and an equally strong impulse to throw her brush at him. It wasn't a matter of being self-conscious about her body. Good grief, her tank top and briefs were more concealing than what women wore on the beaches these days. But just because she didn't have her draperies and blinds yet, did that give him a right to invade her privacy like some voyeur?

Well, he'd picked on the wrong woman if he thought he could intimidate her this time, in her own *home*. Losing A.J. had forced her to toughen up in a great number of ways. She knew how to stand up for herself and not let anyone boss, shame or bully her.

With indignation and fury building, she matched him stare for stare. She could almost feel his gaze shift and linger. Never had she met anyone with such audacity.

"You won't intimidate me again," she muttered, fuming.

But her defiance didn't have much effect on him, either. The only movement came from the birds flying between their houses in search of breakfast for themselves and their hatchlings. Cardinals, chickadees, wrens and bluebirds sailed by, singing their praises of the May sunshine. Farther off she heard a woodpecker work diligently at a dead pine tree; the staccato, hollow tapping that came through the screen echoed the pulse pounding in her throat and at her temples. All that sweet innocence only made the broad-shouldered shadowy figure next door all the more surreal, and menacing.

Feeling her confidence wavering, she tossed her brush onto the counter. Back in the bedroom she grabbed her leggings, and shoes, and shot through the doorway. Awful, awful man, she seethed, stomping down the stairs. She wished her bare feet and modest weight created the thunderous acoustics that her annoyance craved. Did he sleep by that confounded computer? Was this what she had to look forward to from having him as a neighbor?

To think she'd been so pleased to have double windows in the master bedroom. It meant she could better enjoy the view of the ancient wisteria that rose from Zachary Denton's backyard and nearly engulfed everything in its path as it crept over fences and trees in search of sunlight. Bad enough to have missed this year's blooms; was she going to have to keep everything tightly shut and lose the view altogether? It wasn't right. It wasn't fair!

Downstairs she dropped her things by her new telephone and angrily stepped into her leggings and shoes, then jerked open the front door. She'd give him credit for one thing, though—he'd raised her blood pressure so much she didn't need any caffeine to finish waking up!

Outside, she took a welcome, deep breath of fresh air. Yesterday's rain had soaked everything through and through, and lingering humidity made the air heavy, the grass and shrubbery dew-drenched. The sun peered through the haze, its warmth stirring a potpourri of scents from the countless varieties of wildflowers and trees that flourished in the piney woods of East Texas. Willa let the promising day and the fresh air soothe her. It lasted only until she realized her paper wasn't on the driveway as she'd hoped.

"Not this, too?" Sighing, she checked on the other side of the van in case the delivery boy's aim had been way off.

It wasn't there, either. But as she scanned her yard, she spotted the plastic-bag-enclosed paper tied to her mailbox. Relieved that a black cloud of bad luck wasn't settling in over her house after all, she went to retrieve it.

Easier said than done, she decided, realizing how well the boy had secured the thing to her mailbox. She had to tug hard to free it, and the force of the move jerked open the aluminum box's lid. Inside, was a folded sheet of letter-size paper.

"Oh, happy day," she drawled, almost amused. She hadn't even finished moving in yet and already she was the recipient of her first piece of junk mail.

Curious to know who had been this ambitious, she drew out the paper and unfolded it.

It wasn't an advertisement, and for a moment she frowned down at the cut-out, odd-shaped letters from magazines and newspapers that had been glued unevenly to the sheet. Her mind simply refused to make sense of it.

"Too tempting for words."

What on earth was this? Who would put something so ridiculous and—

The nerve! Oh, yes, she understood now. Did he think she wouldn't be able to put two and two together? From what she could tell of the few other residents who lived farther down the road, they were either elderly or working people with no children. Hardly the type to indulge in such a tasteless gesture. But she had no such confidence in her nearest neighbor.

What had been his plan? Did he think she was going to be fooled into believing the Vilary stalker had chosen her as his next victim? It would serve him right if she phoned the police this minute and turned him in. Let him explain away his unbalanced behavior to them!

But that would probably bring every reporter in the state upon them like a swarm of those killer bees said to be invading from South America. Willa drew her lower lip between her teeth. No way did she want to cope with something like that. She was no recluse, but the ads and interviews she occasionally did for her store was enough "media" for her. In comparison the press who'd haunted her every step after A.J.'s employer had tried to blame his crash on pilot error had been like being chased by a pack of starving wild dogs.

Her resentment growing, she eyed Zachary Denton's house. No, she didn't want to go over there again; however, she would. She could handle this herself, *and* enjoy it! Let him have a taste of what it was like to be threatened.

She underhanded her newspaper in the direction of her front door, and this time used the street to reach Zachary Denton's front walk. It wasn't a much better choice than the tall weeds, though. Maybe she'd avoided the ticks and chiggers this way, but the number of potholes made the trip a different challenge. Thanks to yesterday's flooding, every one of them was brimming with muddy water. Apparently the county road department didn't like him, either.

By the time she reached his porch, her once pristine jogging shoes and leggings were splattered with East Texas red clay. Disgusted, she pounded on the screen door.

"Don't you dare ignore me!" She glared up at the unblinking eye targeted on her. "Open up or this goes to the press."

She held up the sheet of paper to the camera. Several long seconds later she heard the inside latch give. Telling herself that she had to ignore the responding lurch from her stomach, Willa stormed inside.

He sat where she'd found him yesterday, at the top of the stairs, looking like an exiled dictator of some ragtag country who was in a particularly bad mood. She eyed him with disdain. Whatever the man spent his money on, it certainly wasn't clothes and razor blades.

Intent on giving him a taste of his own medicine and making him as agitated as he'd made her, she quickly started up the stairs. She knew better than to dwell on the wisdom of the move—or rather, the lack thereof. This had to do with principle.

"What do you think you're doing?"

Although his dark, almost wild gaze had the sharpness of a spear lancing through her, she shot back, "I'll do the talking this time."

"Not if I decide to call the police and have you arrested for harassment and trespassing."

"Good idea. Call them! I can't wait to hear you explain away *this*."

"Let me see that!"

With impressive control and speed, he leaned forward and, before she could stop him, he snatched the paper out of her grasp. Afraid he meant to shred it, Willa considered trying to get it back, but she didn't want to risk destroying it herself. Checking her impulse, she attempted to ignore her sudden disadvantage by studying her strange neighbor from this closer vantage point.

At least he looked somewhat less unkempt this morning, although he still hadn't shaved, and his eyes were as bloodshot as ever. Finding that they were gray surprised her. She'd expected the same opaque brown of his hair and beard, a shade that in certain light people was often mistaken for black. Then again, the gray was opaque and nearly black, too. And so was his mood, she noted as he shot her a brief, sharp glare.

What a big, fierce man. He looked perfectly capable of launching himself out of that wheelchair and strangling the life out of her; in fact, his hands weren't anything close to what she'd pictured for a writer. No long, elegant piano fingers here. Zachary Denton's hands were closer to paws: huge, thick-fingered and callused like a laborer's. She knew the latter was from wheeling his chair, but it reminded her of what A.J. used to say about Denton's work. *He writes like a man's man.*

What a crazy thing to remember. She'd never quite understood what A.J. had meant, either. In fact she'd argued to him how silly the comment was, insisting that no woman had ever declared a member of her sex, "a woman's woman."

However, as she watched the broken, but still-powerful man before her sweep a hand through his thick wavy mane, her increasingly rebellious imagination kicked into gear and suddenly she understood the macho thing. She could visualize how Zachary Denton's hands would look caressing a woman's body...how they would feel.

No, not just any female body. Hers.

She gripped the railing more tightly and looked away as an irrepressible quiver centered deep inside her.

"I warned you," he said, his tone never more grim.

She glanced back in time to see him suck in a deep breath, his broad chest swelling, until it seemed almost too much for the seams of the cleaner, but ancient, black T-shirt. No surprise when even his pale but well-developed biceps were at least twice the size of hers. "Wh-what?"

"You heard me. If you'd listened, this would never have happened."

Willa was glad for the subtle insult; it served to get her mind back on business all the faster. "Nice try but no Oscar, Mr. Denton. I know this is your doing."

"Are you nuts?"

"No. But you are if you think you're going to get away with it."

"Lady," he ground out, his glare all but impaling her, "in case you haven't noticed, this is a *wheelchair.*"

"Which proves nothing."

For an instant he looked genuinely dumbfounded, but the rage quickly returned, stronger and more explosive than before. "Excuse me all to hell, but this thing doesn't come with a certificate qualifying me to be in it. You'll just have to take my word that when you crash-land a single-engine plane, flipping it twice, there's a good reason to believe the doctors when they tell you you're in this thing for the rest of your stinking life!"

No one had ever yelled at her before, at least not quite like this. Between her shock and the sickly feeling that came as he described his living nightmare, she reached for the last shreds of her patience. "With all due respect, Mr. Denton—"

"Let's get something straight, *Mrs.* Whitney, you have no more respect for me than I have for you."

Unfortunately, that was proving true, but the remark still stung. "Fine. Then let's get down to the bottom line, shall we? I'm here and plan to stay, and I'd better not find anything like this in my mailbox again." She snatched back the paper.

Sun-dried rawhide couldn't have stretched any tighter than the muscles on his square-jawed face. "Did you see any mud trail from my house to yours? Any on the porch ramp?"

"No," she admitted reluctantly. What's more, it had stopped raining early in the evening.

"And there isn't any mud on my tires now, is there? So what makes you all-fired certain I did that?"

He had to ask that? After yesterday? "There's no one else," she replied, struggling to keep from letting him spook her again.

"Really." Once again his gaze swept over her, lingering on her breasts. "I think you're forgetting one crucial point."

She couldn't understand how someone in his condition could turn a simple comment into such an insult. Barely able to stay put, Willa replied, "What?"

"Some nut case is out there stalking local women."

Willa wouldn't buy it. "I think you'd like me to believe this is connected with that. But I find it more than slightly suspicious that after living in Vilary for nearly six years, operating a successful shop in a busy mall and having my photograph in the local paper any number of times, it's only when I move in next to *you* that this happens."

"Maybe the stalker does know about you and your sexy lingerie business," Zachary Denton countered with a smile that didn't quite reach his eyes. "Maybe he's just been saving you for something special."

CHAPTER FOUR

Willa felt certain someone or something was sucking the air out of the room. Had Zachary Denton triggered another of his ingenuous contraptions, or was he a true fan of hypnotism and testing his skills on her? Whatever the case, she had to open her mouth to get any air into her lungs.

"How do you know about what's in my store?"

"Maybe I'm psychic."

"You think mocking me is going to resolve anything?"

"Who says I'm mocking you? At any rate, when you storm into a man's house, you take what you get." When she opened her mouth to protest, he gestured for her to save her breath. "All right, you said it yourself, you've been in the paper...and as I told you before, when something happens around here that may affect me, I ask questions."

"A reasonable explanation."

"You mean this is the start of a beautiful friendship?"

"At least a civil coexistence if you'll finally admit this." Willa held up the note again. "Because I still think you did it."

"Go away, Mrs. Whitney. Go home and lock your doors, because I may be a lot of things, including half-mad. But most of all, I'm no gentleman, and I'm damned tired of pretending for you."

Hoping he couldn't see her knees trembling, she nodded. "I'm going. But consider this my final warning. Anything more and I'm going straight to the police."

His face turned a deep red, his eyes feverish. "If I were you, I'd put up some curtains on my windows first. You wouldn't want our boys in blue jumping to the conclusion that lonely, young widows who prance around practically naked deserve what they get."

Until this instant, she'd never wanted to commit physical violence before, and considering the size and build of the man, if she tried it, no doubt she would end up with a broken hand...or neck. But it might be worth it.

For pity's sake, he's turning you into a barbarian!

"To think my husband used to rave about your work," she whispered, her throat raw from tears she'd choke on before spilling. "You're worse than pitiful. You're disgusting."

"And you're a tease!" A new, almost satanic gleam lit his eyes. The mouth that should have been tender, even passionate, twisted cruelly. "But you'd better be careful. Apparently you haven't noticed a pattern with the stalker."

The more he mentioned the dreaded situation, the more she was willing to believe he really knew something. Her tank top began to stick to her back, and she made herself ask, "What pattern?"

"All the women who've been followed have been blondes. They all had blue eyes."

She almost reached up to touch her own hair. "The newspapers haven't reported anything like that, nor has that been stated on TV." She knew. This was the one bit of bad news she *had* been following. All three women had been returning to their homes late at night, and luckily had escaped serious injury. One fainted when the stalker put his gloved hands around her neck. Another managed to knock him off-balance and run. And a neighbor out for an evening stroll saved the third from rape, or worse. But little else had been disclosed. "How do you know this?"

"I told you, I'm psychic."

She didn't know whether to believe him or not. "If you know anything, you have to tell the authorities."

"No."

She couldn't believe his resolute rejection. *He* was worse than a barbarian. "You must! How can you even consider not telling them?"

"That's my business. In any case, if the authorities haven't already picked up on the pattern, they deserve to be fired."

"Don't those women deserve something? What are you waiting for? He might rape or kill the next one!" She had to be caught up in some incredible nightmare. Befuddled, Willa rubbed at her forehead and searched for some way to reach him. "If you could help some-one, save someone, wouldn't you want to do that?"

"I've tried, but the lady chooses not to hear me."

He was referring to her—she understood that much—but *was* it a warning or threat? "I can't not pass this on. You can play your mind games, but the police— Oh!"

She'd begun to turn around, intent on getting out of there, but she'd underestimated Zachary Denton's speed and reach. As he closed his hand around her wrist and jerked her back, she knew she'd said too much, and now there would be hell to pay.

The note sailed out of her grasp. *She* went sprawling across his lap. The force of her fall sent his chair rolling back a few feet until it thudded to a stop against the wrought-iron elevator cage.

Eye to eye with her captor, she tried to focus, tried to catch her breath...tried not to notice the fierce pain in her left thigh from striking the chair's arm, tried not to notice his powerful muscles bunching beneath her hand, and beneath them the strong beat of his heart. She failed on all counts.

Not only did she have to deal with a sudden, debilitating fear, the longer their gazes stayed locked, the more she became aware of him as a man. It was impossible. Beyond bizarre, she thought, dazed and edging toward panic when she couldn't free herself.

"Let me go."

"When I'm ready."

What did that mean? What was next? Was he going to fling her down the stairs? He had the strength. The only question was whether he possessed the brutality.

But something other than violence transformed the whiskered pale face so close to hers. To her amazement his gunmetal-gray eyes almost cleared of haunted shadows and secrets, and taking its place came emotions she wasn't prepared for. Wonder...concern...regret...all proved shocking enough. But desire?

At first she thought she might have struck her head on the banister and was imagining it. Intent on focusing on the pain their collision must have caused, she was about to insist he let her up. Then she felt the unmistakable, physical stirring against her hip.

Neither of them moved. Trapped and vulnerable, she could only wait, and watch the wide, well-formed mouth so frighteningly close. Wait and wonder. Would his kiss be hard and rough, or slow and hungry? How far did he intend to go? Would she survive it?

"My God, you're lovely."

His gaze shifted to *her* lips. Her mouth went dry as he slid a hand up her back, beneath the fall of her hair. Strong fingers molded themselves around her nape... and slowly, slowly he drew her toward him.

You're going to let this happen?

"Zach? Yo, man!"

Willa started at the sound of the unexpected, but strangely familiar voice rising from below. Someone was at the front door! She began to glance around, but Zachary Denton tightened his grip, keeping her still. As he moved his hand from her nape to her throat, those emotions that had almost seduced her receded, and back came the secretive shadows and the glint of violence.

She swallowed, but afraid to make a mistake, waited for him to make his decision.

"Hey, you all right? I'm coming in, okay?" the visitor shouted upon hearing no response.

Before the screen door opened, Zachary Denton lifted her back onto her feet. Surprised, Willa steadied herself by holding onto his forearms. They were hot steel against her fingers.

"Go. Say nothing to him."

Although he spoke calmly, he looked paler than ever. Drained. But eager to put some distance between them, Willa didn't dwell on that; instead, she hurried down the stairs. She didn't remember the note until she approached the bottom, and spun around in time to see him tucking it into his T-shirt's single pocket.

"Whoa! Sorry, man. Did I mess up on the time or something?"

Ignoring the man who'd just noticed her, Willa hesitated. Did she make a scene and demand her property back or leave as he'd said? Blast him for being so enigmatic.

Leave!

Zachary Denton's intense look projected as strong a message as any verbal command. "I was just going," she said to the newcomer as she hurried down the rest of the stairs. But disgusted with herself for losing the note and more, Willa could only nod toward the blond giant who appeared as embarrassed as he did curious.

Like Zachary Denton, the newcomer was a well-toned product that bespoke hours of extensive and disciplined weight training; and if she hadn't recognized him, the Vilary Vantage Health Club and Spa logo on his T-shirt would have identified him. He was one of the trainers. The one with the neon smile and a cavalier's manners, she recalled, remembering how he often ran to open the doors for the health club's female clientele. Even her oldest saleswoman, sensible Sophia, grew all breathless and giddy when he strolled by Whimsy.

"I know you."

So much for thinking she could escape without small talk. Willa nodded politely. "Hi." She knew she owed this man with the model-perfect tan a debt a gratitude, but with Zachary Denton's warning echoing in her mind, she wanted desperately to get out of there. "I'm the new neighbor," she offered reluctantly, hooking her thumb in the direction of her house. "Willa Whitney. I came over to introduce myself."

Youthful features puckered into a slight frown, making him look no more than a year or two her senior. "Couldn't help but wonder seeing as the door's rarely open. He doesn't like visitors."

The conspiratorial whisper came as the custom-made

elevator cranked into operation, and Willa stiffened. "He's made that abundantly clear."

"Don't take it personally. He's had a rough time of it." Glancing across the foyer as the elevator settled on the ground floor, his gaze grew troubled, almost sad. "You should've seen him before I started working with him."

"You've done wonders with keeping him in shape." *Too bad you can't do something with what's going on beneath that wild mane of hair.* "It's…Greg, right?" she added, trying to recall what the girls at the store had called him.

"Ger. Ger Sacks. Sounds less nerdy than Gerald." He grinned and shrugged. "I like your store. Crazy stuff you peddle."

So much for hoping he'd confused her with someone else. She didn't know if she liked the idea of her merchandise being described as "crazy," but Willa murmured her thanks, adding, "Well, after you prime the bodies, they want some nice things to show off the results." Her gaze drifted beyond him as Zachary Denton wheeled out of the metal cage and rolled himself toward them. Feeling his eyes like two drills boring into her, she began backing away. "Um…I really have to run. Nice to finally meet you, Ger."

"Ditto. Come see me some time. Not that you need it," he added with a brief, sweeping glance, "but everyone could use a little cardiovascular workout once in a while."

"True, but I get that by doing all of my own housework."

She did run then, all the way back home, not stopping until she had her front door locked and bolted behind her. Only when she slumped against the sturdy wood did she think about what had happened.

Had the combination of Zachary Denton's accident and his work driven him to the edge of madness? If so, he'd at least been sane enough to outmaneuver her and get that note. Why did he want it if he hadn't been the one to put it in her box? And is that why he'd almost kissed her? Oh, God, that was the most incredible of all—she was *disappointed* it hadn't happened.

Blue-eyed blondes. Just like her.

My God you're lovely.

Blondes...blondes...blondes...

Willa covered her face with her hands. Dear Heaven, what had she gotten herself into?

"You're tight."

"And I plan to get tighter," Zach replied, thinking of the stiff drink he would pour himself as soon as he sent his trainer on his way.

Not bothering to open his eyes, he willed the strong, capable hands massaging the knots and kinks out of his back to work their magic—but faster. At least the guy was good. Gerald Sacks wasn't a fully-trained masseur; however, he was more than adequate, and most important, he saved Zach from having to deal with yet another person intruding on his space and privacy.

"You keep pouring all that booze into yourself and pretty soon you won't need me anymore, you'll need a mortician."

"Anytime you figure you no longer want my money, say the word. Then you won't have to watch." Zach had no intention of taking that kind of bull from anyone. Not even Felix who had been his agent since the start—

well before his first-class trip through hell—had permission to lecture him.

"Sorry."

Hearing the mumbled word and sensing the hurt beneath it, Zach realized what a mistake he'd made. A stupid one. He needed to stop remembering the scene of Willa talking to Sacks, not to mention replaying the moment he'd almost learned the taste and feel of her, and keep his mind on the business at hand.

After a grunt and an oath, he added, "Ignore me. Too many hours at the computer lately." That much was true. His body ached from the ninety-minute workout Ger had put him through.

"I know. Your neck and shoulders are a mess, man." As if wanting to make his point, he gave a surprisingly painful twist to the muscle he'd been working.

"Son of a...*hey!*" Zach lifted himself on his elbows and glared at the man who gazed back at him through startled, summer-blue eyes. "It's the legs that have the nerve damage! What are you trying to do, kill me?"

Ger's expression turned as studious as when he was teaching a new move. "Killing wouldn't take that much strength. When I was into martial arts, I learned that much. And I was only trying to make the point that you ignored technique today. Injure yourself, you'll be hurting more than you. Think about my reputation, man."

Zach doubted he'd ever heard Ger say anything half as intelligent, and the revelation about his past was interesting, as well. Wondering how else he'd underestimated him, he lowered himself back to the towel-covered table. "You studied martial arts?"

"Hell, no. I took a few classes and found out it wasn't for me."

"Why not?"

"Just wasn't. Too much head stuff." Ger paused to pour more lotion into his palm. "You want more work on your shoulders or do you want me to move on?"

"Finish. I have to get back upstairs."

In the sixteen months since he'd hired Gerald Sacks to transform the den into a training room and keep his body from atrophying, they'd had their moments of tension and disagreement. The accident had honed Zach's innate tendencies to be strong-willed and acerbic. What's more, the soft-spoken, machine-tanned Ger was one of only three people who could gain entrance into the house, and was damned well paid for his time and service. Zach figured that gave *him* the right not to mince words, and pretend to be something he wasn't.

"You want to talk?"

Sometimes Zach did tire of his isolation, and the singular cerebral focus of writing; and as with the chess games he looked forward to with Roger Elias, he saw conversation as a discipline requiring skill and strategy. But although Ger was a good source of information for what was going on in town, he wasn't exactly the most inspiring, let alone challenging, conversationalist. Then again, Zach thought as his thoughts darkened, political or philosophical insight wasn't what he wanted from his trainer.

"Talk about what?"

"The underwear lady. Her coming over the way she did."

He grunted. Wouldn't Willa love hearing herself described that way? "From what I've seen in newspaper advertisements, 'underwear' doesn't quite describe what she sells."

Ger made no response to that, but after several long seconds, he ventured with some caution. "I, uh, thought since she kinda looks like...you know, it might have upset you.''

Renewed tension created the coldest knot yet in Zach's belly. "Do you think she looks like my ex-wife?" he mumbled into his pillowed towel.

His trainer had been here the last time less-than-beloved Judith had slithered in seeking more money. As usual, the scene had gone from drolly amusing to ugly, thanks to the woman's vicious mouth. By the time she left, Zach thought her lucky to escape with only a scratch on her chin from the car keys he'd flung back at her.

How he despised the woman. Despise? Hell, he hated her with every ounce of his being. Not because she'd filed an assault case against him after their argument when he'd told her he was filing for a divorce, or for taking so much that wasn't hers, but for unleashing the demons inside him. The demons that whispered he *could* commit murder.

"Well, maybe not up close." Ger sounded sorry to have brought up the subject. Moving down to concentrate on Zach's legs, he continued, "I mean, I know Ju—uh, Mrs. D. is older. Maybe I thought that because they're about the same height and build."

And that was all Willa had in common with his ex-wife, Zach thought. When he'd touched Willa, and looked into her eyes, he'd seen a soul and not a heartless, conniving she-devil.

"Don't forget the hair," he drawled, curious to hear what else Ger might say. He already knew, however, that Willa's glorious coloring didn't come out of a bottle. "And the blue eyes."

"Oh. Okay. I hadn't noticed."

Disappointed, Zach closed his eyes. As far as he was concerned, the conversation was over.

"Say…" Ger's laugh sounded almost like a girl's giggle. "I just had a thought. Wouldn't it be weird if the stalker got rid of your ex old lady for you?"

Zach opened his eyes and briefly focused on the note sticking out of the T-shirt he'd hung on the doorknob. Then he thought of the several others upstairs in his desk.

"I hope not," he replied, tempering the savagery stirring inside him. "If anyone's going to give Judith a tour of hell, it's going to be me."

CHAPTER FIVE

On Sunday, Zach was still dropping bombshells...and still groping in the dark.

"Would you mind repeating that?"

He recognized the ominous, chilly tone in Felix Fraser's voice, but it didn't keep him from pouring himself another Scotch from the bottle he kept on the corner of his desk. Swirling the melting ices cubes in the amber liquid, Zach took a sip, recalling a time right after the crash when he'd witnessed Felix's Arctic-Attitude directed at Judith, who'd burst into his hospital room and pretended concern. It was the same frigidity he'd heard countless times since, when his agent negotiated with publishers, movie producers and audio rights reps. But this was the first time Zach had found himself on the receiving end of it.

He found it oddly enjoyable.

"You heard me." Turning back to the computer screen, he eyed the last page of the chapter he'd finished only minutes ago. Two chapters in two days, not bad. "I've put off doing *Under the City* right now. I want to pursue another idea."

"But Carstairs is expecting *City* by Christmas" came the steel-coated-by-velvet reply. "They've issued a press release to that effect. Your readers are expecting *Under the City*."

"And they'll get it. But not yet."

"When then?"

"After *Checkmate*."

He could picture Felix, an elegant fifty-seven-year-old, tall, large-boned man, pinching the bridge of his El Greco nose as he fought for control of his temper. It was the curse of Felix's Spanish, Scottish and Russian genes to be eternally at war with himself. He'd simply inherited too much passion, even for his six-foot-four-inch frame.

"Lord almighty, Zach. Why don't you simply take a stake and drive it through my chest? Exactly what the—" Pausing just in time to censor a particularly crude expletive because, like an alcoholic, once Felix started swearing it was difficult for him to stop, he drew in a deep breath and started over. "What is *Checkmate?*"

"Only a fine madness right now." The liquor was beginning to ease the fatigue, tension and pain in his body, and allowed Zach to indulge in an evil grin. "Primarily because I don't know how it ends yet."

"I see. What about the premise? Do you have a clue about that?"

The snideness was vintage Fraser, as well. The Houston literary agent was more than a fascinating, enigmatic study as a businessman; one-on-one he usually exuded a theatrically affected persona. Zach hadn't been able to resist using him in his work before, but as a composite character. Never the man as a whole. He knew Felix would enjoy being immortalized in print, and wondered how much to hint that it might just happen, and soon.

"A clue...all right. Call it three stories in one. A project like nothing I've ever done before."

"That's what *Under the City* is supposed to be, and if you remember correctly, I had to practically prostrate myself before Carstairs to stop his complaining about the young antagonists in the story.''

Zach could think of a few tongue-in-cheek responses to the idea that Felix would prostrate himself to anyone, but decided to leave well enough alone. He hadn't called his agent to make more trouble for himself than necessary. First and foremost, he was on a fishing expedition.

''Just hear me out,'' he replied, attempting to sound believably entreating. ''It's a story, inside a story, inside a story. A play for revenge, and power and the sacrifice of innocence. Only—'' he swung his chair around to see if his comely neighbor had finished hanging the blinds in her bedroom ''—I'm not sure yet how much the innocent will have to sacrifice.''

Felix's responding sigh stretched like a full-grown python across the wires. ''I don't need this, Zach. I just saw you Friday night. You said nothing about switching story lines.''

''You didn't ask. If you'll recall, you were on your way in from a meeting in Dallas and merely 'stopping by to check on your favorite client,' *and* a bit of my premium whiskey. You were unwinding and in no mood to talk shop.''

''Well, I am now,'' Felix snapped, clearly irritated that he'd missed the opportunity to catch on to this sooner. ''And if you had anything close to a conscience, you would have brought up the matter yourself!''

In the pregnant pause that followed, Zach watched Willa frowning over the instructions for the blinds. A part of him would be sorry to see them go up. Another part, less enthusiastic, but rational, knew it was necessary to her survival—and his sanity. What was left of it.

"Zach? Don't you hang up on me."

"When have I ever done that, Felix?" he asked mildly, admiring the subtle curves and valleys he'd held against him only hours before.

"That's true. And I wish you'd be as professional about this commitment. Leave the machinations for your board games with your young chess friend, and write me a nice, scare-the-pants-off-everyone horror story. You know that's what your readers want from you."

"They *want* the next Zachary Denton release…and trust me, it'll be a page-turner. I'm not even sure I'll survive it."

"What's that supposed to mean? Zach? Put that damned glass down for a minute and talk to me!"

"Don't tell me what to do, Felix," Zach warned, instantly serious. "The moment you hear my voice slur, you can preach and demand all you want, but until then butt out."

"Bloody hell, Zach. Since the accident it's been nothing but an uphill battle trying to tiptoe around your black moods and self-destructiveness. You know I've sympathized with your tragedy, defended you as your aversion to do publicity intensified. If that was me in that chair, I wouldn't want to deal with TV cameras and reporters, either. But between your drinking and this neurotic reclusiveness—"

"Be very careful what you say next," he warned his agent in a near whisper.

"Someone needs to say it, and it's past time. Sweet heaven, Zach, sometimes I think we'd all be better off if you'd ridden that damn plane straight into the ground. It might have been kinder than having to watch you destroy yourself this way."

Zach shut his eyes, but there was no stopping the rush of memories Felix's words triggered...the sickening moment when he'd realized the plane had been sabotaged...the shock and the terror...the vow of revenge and the petrified prayer he'd repeated again and again through clenched teeth as he'd bartered for his soul and fought for his life.

When he reopened his eyes, he saw Willa had succeeded in getting the first blind up. He watched shapely calves, knees, then thighs appear, as she tested it, and almost sighed with relief as the red flames of madness receded.

What *was* she wearing beneath that man's dress shirt? And beneath her obvious fear this morning, had the curiosity, even desire he'd seen in those bottomless eyes of hers, been real? The blinds suggested one answer, but he wondered. Were they going up to protect her from him...or to protect her from herself?

Did he want either of them to discover the answer?

"Zach? Zach!"

"I'm here."

"I didn't mean it."

"Oh, but you did." He drew a deep, relaxing breath. "I've never asked you to like me or even to respect what I do, Felix. But I don't pay you to lie to me."

"You're right." Felix's voice flowed heavy with regret. For once, all pretense and affectation vanished. "We need to talk about this. I don't know how much more I can take. I don't even know if I have the guts to break this to Carstairs. We have a *contract* for crying out loud. He could crucify us."

The blinds lifted the rest of the way, and finally she saw him. He'd swept back the sheers to make it easy for her, although it was almost eight in the evening and new storm clouds made it darker than usual for a late spring night. He hadn't turned on the lights, either. No need to remove all the challenge. There was only the glow from the computer screen to let her know he was there. He knew it cast him in an eerie silhouette. Visible, but not identifiable. Real and surreal. As he was.

The unexpected flash in the corner of his right eye stung. It came from the car pulling into his driveway. Round three, he thought, his mood sinking once more.

"Zach, talk to me."

"I have to go, Felix. Young Elias has arrived."

"Let him wait. Why you waste your time with that overambitious weasel is beyond me. He doesn't have any real talent."

"I disagree," Zach replied, refocusing on Willa's frozen stance. "At any rate, it's not wise to underestimate. Anyone. I'll call you soon."

He hung up the phone and after punching the proper button on the remote control to release the downstairs lock, he watched as she hesitantly moved closer to the window to see his visitor more clearly. Despite the distance between them, her confusion and wariness were palpable.

Truly lovely.

The underwear lady, indeed.

What was he going to do about her?

When Zachary Denton left the upstairs room to see to his visitor, Willa lowered her new blinds and shut them tight. Her heart continued to pound from the way he'd been watching her, and seeing the unrecognizable car pull into his driveway hadn't helped. For an unsociable person, Zachary Denton had his share of company.

Stepping back, she considered her workmanship. Not bad for a woman who, only a few years ago, could barely read a tape measure, let alone handle a nail and hammer. Being on one's own certainly forced a person to adapt and try new things, and Willa was glad she'd decided to stick with the same ivory color as the walls. She would use color through accents; she'd chosen green and yellow to go with the sunflower print bedspread and curtains bagged and waiting in the closet.

One more day and she would have her bed again. She rubbed at her aching back. What she wouldn't give to be able to climb into the tub right now. But she wasn't finished with her work for the day. Besides, Starla said she would—

The doorbell sounded, and Willa's thudding heart nearly leapt into her throat. Good grief, a few days around the crown prince of horror and she was turning into a wreck!

Who on earth could it be? She'd just been thinking that Starla said she would call, not stop by. What's more, after getting her number from Kelly, her parents had telephoned from Madrid, which canceled any possibility that they'd concluded their trip early.

Hurrying downstairs, she found herself braking by her purse. Of course, she thought as she realized why. She stooped to dig into the outer pouch. Thank goodness for instincts. She hadn't heard another car stop by except for the one that had pulled into Zachary Denton's driveway; therefore, it would be foolish to answer the door without being prepared.

With her cannister of tear gas in hand, she went to switch on the front lights. Maybe she would leave them on. It might discourage any more funny business from…well, whomever.

Peering through the peephole, she frowned. No one was there.

"Blast." Her nerves didn't need this.

About to go to the front window for a better view, a dark head suddenly popped up out of nowhere. She reared back, but a second later realized who she'd seen.

Starla! Quickly unlocking the dead bolt, she jerked open the door, vowing to herself that as soon as possible she would have a storm door added. Every bit of security would help.

"Starla Donohue, I could shake you!" she cried, stepping aside for her assistant to enter.

Pretty brown eyes tried to look apologetic, but not all the twinkling amber lights dancing in their depths would behave. "Don't be angry with me. I know I said I'd only call, but the suspense got to me. You have to let me have a peek. Look," she grinned, holding up bottle of chardonnay. "I brought a bribe."

Willa shook her head. "But *I* don't have a cork-screw."

The younger woman shook the huge, chic tote bag slung over her shoulder. "Remember this? Since when has anything less than useful emerged from its— Yikes! What's that for?"

She'd finally spotted the tear gas. With a wry smile, Willa shut the door and returned it to her purse. "Over-stretched nerves, obviously. I'll tell you about it in a minute," she added, noting Starla's confusion. "First come have that look around."

Starla's surprise visit gave Willa what she needed— something else to focus on. A good listener with a slightly wacky sense of humor that hid a deeper shy-ness, she reminded Willa of her sister, Kelly, but with longer, golden brown hair, and a softer, rounded figure.

"This place is darling! Not too big to keep up, but large enough not to give you claustrophobia. Like a certain efficiency apartment I could tell you about," she added as an aside. "And it's obvious you've been working your butt off. Oh, wow!" They entered the kitchen where brick and copper created a warm, welcoming environment. "I can't wait to see how you decorate everything. If it turns out half as good as Whimsy did, the paper's going to want to do another feature on you."

Willa hadn't considered that. "I'm not sure I want to share this with the public," she replied, frowning as she retrieved two paper cups from a basket of supplies on the counter.

"You're kidding! Ms. My Life's An Open Book?"

Was she like that? Well, once upon a time maybe, and mostly because A.J.'s stressful work as an emergency helicopter pilot had created a need for counterbalance. More. Relief. His preference had been to throw impromptu, open-house parties. But if truth be known, she would have been happier to have spent those nights cozily in front of a fire, with a romantic dinner and a more romantic bubble bath waiting. Nowadays she had plenty of opportunity to do just that, but without A.J.

"I'm sorry, Willa. What did I say? I didn't mean to dig up ghosts or anything."

"Don't worry about it," she replied, smiling as she presented the cups. "You reminded me that I may have some new decisions to make, that's all."

"Tomorrow's the big day, huh? Ready or not, you're a homeowner again."

She nodded, regaining some of her excitement. "The movers tell me they'll be at the apartment at nine. Are you getting tired of playing chief, cook and bottle washer yet?" she asked, aware of the responsibility she'd placed on her friend's shoulders. Four years her junior, Starla was capable, but young for the pressures Willa knew could come swiftly and without warning.

"To be honest...? As good a time as I'm having, I'd prefer it if you were there." Starla's dimples deepened. "Because I miss our chats like heck. Not having had any brothers and sisters, or being very close to my folks, I guess you've become like an older sister to me. Hope you don't mind."

"Of course I don't mind. I feel the same way about you." Willa hugged her, touched by her friend's admission.

"But I know this is good for me, and that I need to learn to flex my administrative muscles."

"That's a girl! I know you can do it." Willa watched the younger woman ease the cork out the bottle's neck. The pop underscored her pleasure and gratitude that Starla had stopped by after all. "And it's not as if I'm far away. If you can hang on until Tuesday...?"

"Don't worry. We'll be fine." Starla poured the wine. "Now let's change the subject before we get too mushy and sentimental, and wind up with raccoon eyes."

They laughed and touched their cups together. Then Starla reported on the day's sales and reassured Willa that she'd locked the cash and receipts in the small office safe.

"It sounds as if you have everything under control," Willa said, leading the way out of the kitchen again. "Come on and I'll show you the rest of the place." But she was surprised when Starla stopped her at the foot of the stairs.

"Wait. First tell me what's going on? Why the tear

gas?'' She held up a hand the instant Willa hesitated. ''Unless it's pushing the boundaries of our friendship.''

''Don't be silly.'' It surprised and dismayed Willa that Starla could think that, and she told her so.

Once again beaming, her young friend replied, ''Good. Then what is it? Is being on a dead-end street and practically in the woods more to handle than you'd expected?''

Willa sipped her wine, considering the possibility again. ''No, I really enjoy that. There are so many birds, and this evening I glimpsed a deer in my backyard. I can't wait to put up some feeders, and maybe set out something for the deer, too.''

''Now *that* sounds like you.'' Warming to her subject, Starla tilted her head, continuing, ''And I think you'd have to have a good reason to be feeling threatened enough to reach for that stuff in here, so out with it. What's wrong?''

CHAPTER SIX

Willa nibbled at the rim of her cup. "Promise not to laugh?"

"There's nothing funny about tear gas."

"Okay, then don't blow what I say out of proportion, either."

Starla rested an elbow on the banister. "That's not a reassuring way to start this conversation, boss dear. *I'm* the one who's supposed to take the long route to get to the point. You're the one who's always known your own mind—along with everyone else's."

The compliment was nice to hear, despite her doubts about its current accuracy. Willa took a deep breath. "Something's happened that shook me up a bit."

She proceeded to tell her friend about the note—for the moment preferring to leave out what had occurred the day before. As she feared, Starla went from concerned to upset.

"That's too spooky. And I can't *believe* you didn't tell me this when we talked on the phone!" Starla's expression matched her accusatory tone.

"How do you share something like that over the phone?"

"Well, okay. What did the police say?"

Now came the hard part. Willa glanced toward the dining room window, too late realizing what a reflexive move that was becoming. "I didn't call them."

As expected, Starla was aghast. "Why on earth not? There's a creep out there who's terrifying almost every

woman in this town. You mean to tell me that note
didn't make you think of him?''

"You didn't let me finish." Only then did Willa realize she would share everything—or almost everything.
Maybe, she decided, it was time to get someone else's
input. "Remember who I said I'll be having as a neighbor?''

"Who could forget? I was about to ask you if—''
Her assistant's eyes went so wide, they could almost
have been used as dual makeup mirrors. "You
think…*Zachary Denton?*''

"I don't know," Willa admitted, knowing it would
have sounded crazy to her if Starla had been the one
presenting such a bombshell. Once again, feeling un-
characteristically unsure of herself, she took a sip of her
wine.

"Willa, isn't he completely disabled or something?''

"He uses a wheelchair, but he's hardly disabled.''
Images of Zachary Denton, flashbacks of his speed and
strength, played out before her eyes, leaving her uncom-
fortably warm. She fingered the damp hairs at her nape
that had slipped free of her ponytail. "His house is set
up to accommodate the chair—there are ramps, and
some electric gizmos. He even has an elevator. Believe
me, getting around isn't a problem for him.''

To her credit, Starla didn't miss a beat. Narrowing
her eyes, which gave her rounded face an almost Eastern quality, she demanded, "How do you know that?''

"I went over there.''

"You didn't!''

"Well, think about it," Willa insisted, holding fast
to the logic that had ruled back then. "Isn't it a bit
suspicious how nothing like that had happened to me
until I start moving in here? How many times have I

been one of the last people to leave the mall at night? Have you ever heard that I've had any real problems. Oh, sure, a few of the high school boys drive by getting revved up for their next ball game and hoot and holler a bit. But that's all.''

"Willa, we're not talking about high school kids, we're talking about *Zachary Denton*...and to take matters into your own hands and confront him like that.'' Starla looked upward and shook her head. "Bet he was thrilled with your accusation.''

"I'm fairly certain I won't be getting a Christmas card from him.''

"At least you can still make jokes. I'd be locked in my bedroom closet if this was happening to me.''

"I've had my moments.''

Nodding, her friend glanced in the direction of Zachary Denton's house. Then, as though in a trance, she went to the bay window and leaned against the wall. "I have to ask. Is he still a hunk?''

Willa had forgotten Starla was as devoted a Denton fan as A.J. had been. "I couldn't really tell. I don't think he's shaved or cut his hair in months.''

Starla shot her a dismayed, yet fascinated look over her shoulder. "You mean what the press said is true? He's a hermit? That's so...mysterious.''

"I hate to burst your romantic illusions, but he was rude, threatening and...'' She'd almost said "totally without feeling,'' but the words stuck in her throat because they would have been a lie.

Something sensitive and disturbing *had* surfaced between them. Something so unnerving that it had kept her awake long into the night. When she'd finally slept, she'd dreamed of a great, dark shadow lowering itself over her and shocking her back to a world of awareness she'd been resisting. She'd tried to resist *it*, too, but it had been relentless, seeming to know all her vulnerabilities and desires. Awakening with a start, she'd found herself perspiring and out of breath, as if—

"It's crazy," she moaned, rubbing her forehead. Fighting the restlessness building inside her, she began pacing the gleaming living room floor. "He's complicated, okay? And stranger than anyone I've ever met."

"Strange? You mean as in crazy?"

Willa could tell by the way Starla asked that she didn't want an affirmative answer, and although she felt for her friend, she admitted, "He can give that impression. But in the next minute—" she remembered the feel of his fingers on her neck "—he can be almost gentle. For the most part, though, he's secretive, paranoid and he talks in riddles."

"His life has to be frustrating, being in that wheelchair," Starla insisted, sounding more and more like the devil's advocate. "After all, he was an active, adventurous guy before, and now he can't even…you know."

"Can't he?"

"Well, I'm assuming *that's* out." But Starla eyed her with increasing curiosity. "Are you blushing?"

"What if he can walk?" Willa said returning to her pacing.

"I *wasn't* talking about walking."

"But supposing he can?" She didn't want to deal with the idea that this way she wouldn't have to feel guilty for suspecting him. "He's in great shape from working out. Ger Sacks at the health club works with him."

That drew Starla away from her post, and she made a throaty sound. "Another hunk."

"Think so? Guess what? Zachary Denton has a body

in almost as good shape. In fact…blast, I'm not going to be able to avoid this.''

''Avoid what?''

''He's functional.''

''Excuse me?''

''I think he could…be with a woman if he wanted.''

Once the shock wore off, delight and intrigue lit Starla's animated brown eyes. ''I'm almost afraid to ask, but how did you discover that little tidbit?''

''He became angry with me, and tried to grab the note. I ended up sprawled across him. Believe me, the change was impossible to miss.'' Her throat as dry as her tone, Willa took a longer sip of her wine.

''Wow, that's wild. You and Zachary Denton.''

''There is no me and Zachary Denton!''

Starla lifted an eyebrow. ''Really? So why are you practically scarlet, especially when you never blush? What happened? Did he kiss you?''

''No!''

And she had to deal with her shame for wanting it, for wanting him to take without asking. That was the worst of it. The man was dangerous, and maybe certifiable for all she knew, yet she couldn't stop thinking about those few moments in his arms. No matter how she tried to insist there had also been something deeper, something spiritual in his eyes, she failed. The explosive sexuality between them made a mockery of the idea, and her.

''What are you going to do?'' Starla asked, as if sensing Willa's inner battle.

''What can I do? He has the note. Probably's destroyed it by now. No police officer's going to take me seriously if I make an accusation.'' She shrugged, intensely aware of her precarious situation. ''I'm stuck.

I've invested too much money in this place to try to sell right away. And damn it all, I *like* it here.'' She sighed and lifted her cup in a noble, if shaky, salute to herself. "All I can do is wait and see what happens."

"But, Willa..." Starla bit her lip. "What if it is a coincidence—only a dangerous one? What if you have attracted the attention of the stalker?"

"I have to put my faith in the theory I haven't."

Starla didn't look pleased. "Only this afternoon another employee at the mall told me that she thought she'd been followed Saturday night after work."

"And I heard a psychologist state on the radio that if they don't catch this guy soon, he's liable to do more than stalk and frighten women half to death," Willa admitted, meeting Starla's worried gaze. "He's bound to actually hurt someone. You be extra-careful, too. Okay?"

"Yeah. That's one thing you don't have to tell me twice." Starla glanced back toward Zachary Denton's house. The hint of light behind the draperies suggested activity in one of the first-floor rooms. "Was he home Friday night?"

Willa sighed, wondering who his visitor was, and what was going on in there. "That's the big question. I don't know."

Although he and Roger Elias had a standing appointment for every Wednesday and Sunday, Zach didn't feel like playing chess tonight. But having set his plan in motion, he knew if he wanted it to work, the spider had to keep building his web.

Six months ago he'd advertised for a chess partner— or more accurately, an instructor—and had been disappointed with the results. Apparently not many Texans were into the game, at least not anyone in Vilary. Or so he thought, until Felix brought him a piece of fan mail from an aspiring writer who actually lived in town. What's more, it turned out Elias played chess, but had missed the ad. And although Zach would prefer to eat tabbouleh three times a day rather than critique another writer's work, particularly an oversensitive, unpublished one, he agreed that if the department store manager had something for him to read, he would take a look at it. If there was a shadow of talent to work with, they had a deal.

Now he knew that Felix was wrong about the bookish thirty-year-old. Roger did have talent, coarse and largely untapped, but clearly evident. However, Zach hoped this wasn't going to be one of those nights when the ambitious fledgling wanted feedback. It would be challenge enough to keep focused on the game…well, on both of them.

Roger followed him into the study, and while Zach positioned his chair at his usual spot behind the field of black marble combatants, Roger set his designer leather briefcase beside the couch. Zach indulged in a silent sigh of relief.

The briefcase was as much a part of Roger's uniform as the suit and tie, and his Italian loafers. Practicing a yuppie version of eastern visualization, Roger believed that dressing as a successful writer would serve to make him one that much faster. Thus the case went everywhere he did, and it was only when he set the thing out of reaching distance, that Zach knew he had a reprieve. If Elias had something to share, he would have carried it to the table, much like the poor soul who follows the president, toting the country's defense system codes.

"Help yourself to the bar." Zach wanted a moment to watch the younger man and gauge his mood.

Murmuring his thanks, Roger headed with surprising eagerness to the well-stocked, mahogany armoire, his slacks flapping comically around his broomstick legs. A good thing he was only average height, Zach mused, and not for the first time, otherwise the kid would have looked like one of those walkingsticks that peered at him from the window screens throughout the summer. It didn't help that Roger was also almost as colorless, having been cursed with nondescript brown hair, sallow skin and unremarkable, twitchy features. It was only when you looked beyond the glasses, into his indigo blue eyes, that you picked up on the seriousness and intelligence of the man inside. If he'd been prone to religiousness or politics, he could have been a fanatic. Instead, the demon tormenting his soul was his ambition to be a famous writer.

And an interesting demon it was, Zach thought lifting an eyebrow, as Roger poured himself a particularly generous amount of his V.V.S.O.P. brandy into a snifter. It wasn't the portion that bothered him, it was the reason behind the splurge. Usually, it was all Roger could do to sip his way through a single, weak Scotch and water, and then Zach suspected it was more for appearance' sake than a genuine liking for alcohol.

"Bad day?"

"I'd rather not talk about it." As he approached the table, Roger ran a hand through hair too conservatively short to have been mussed. "If we're going to play, let's play."

Zach was too amused to be offended. "Isn't that my line?" Then he saw the man's face. "What the hell happened to you?"

Between the dim lighting and Roger's protective movements, it was only as he took his seat that Zach saw the raw scrape that went from cheekbone to chin.

"I fell," Roger replied, avoiding Zach's narrow-eyed inspection.

But the hand that set the snifter on the table was unsteady. Growing more intrigued by the minute, Zach murmured, "Whatever you did, at least you did a good job of it. You're not hurt anywhere else, are you?"

"No, you don't have to worry that I'll bleed all over the furniture. It's already scabbed over."

Snide pup. Zach watched him down a good third of the expensive liquid in one inexperienced gulp. "Have I ever voiced a concern about my material possessions?" he asked, relying on the quiet tone and cold smile he knew would have the desired effect on his guest.

It didn't seem possible that the man could grow paler, but he did, and after easing the crystal glass back onto the table, he bowed his head, the image of a guilty schoolboy. "It happened last night, as I came home from work. The light outside my apartment had apparently burned out and...and I slipped on the top stair. Brick," he murmured, touching the raw skin on the left side of his face.

Bull, thought Zach. If that were the truth, he would have indulged in the drinking *last* night, and he'd be long over the shakes. Something more serious than a fall had occurred; the question was, why was he lying about it? Had he gotten into a fight and was too embarrassed to admit it?

"Better be careful. I'd hate to lose my chess instructor."

"At least you'd be spared having to read my crap anymore."

He sounded as pouty as a six-year-old. "Oh, I doubt it," Zach drawled, in no hurry to let the matter drop, or to hurry with their game. "There are plenty more where you came from. They'd be bulldozing dirt into your grave, and I'd already be hounded by requests to take your place."

Wounded, stunned eyes stared at him over the board—and then for a brief flash there was hatred, pure and raging. Zach almost nodded in satisfaction.

As quickly as it came, the temper vanished and Elias refocused on the board. When he reached for a white pawn, he trembled so badly, he almost knocked it over. Withdrawing his hand, he barely managed to choke out, "You're in rare form tonight."

"You know the house rules, Roger. Only one self-serving, embittered bastard allowed in this domicile, and I'm it."

"How inconsiderate of me to forget." This time when the man reached for the brandy, he only shivered after swallowing. "Is this outpouring of compassion my doing, or does it have anything to do with the fact that you're about to lose your privacy?" he asked, as soon as he regained the ability to speak. "Couldn't help but notice the lights on next door. What's the matter? Do your new neighbors have a herd of kids that are already driving you nuts?"

Well, well, Zach mused, finding this increasingly entertaining. His protégé had a temper, and a taste for revenge. That's what he'd been wanting to find out, but he'd expected it to take much longer. That scrape on Elias's face couldn't have occurred at a more opportune moment.

"Don't you know?" he drawled, sitting back and steepling his fingers. "It's a cohort of yours."

The finely aged cognac was working fast; Roger was slow to respond. "Mine?"

"In a manner of speaking. At the mall. Isn't your store near that place called Whimsy something or other?"

"Someone at Willa's is moving next door?"

"Its namesake herself." He watched closely, but saw nothing that would suggest he wasn't chasing an empty hunch, so he decided to ask outright. "You didn't know?"

"No." A brief, incredulous laugh burst from his lips before Roger Elias rubbed at his forehead. "Amazing. I swear it's utterly amazing."

"What?" Zach asked, perplexed.

"You. Your luck. You write a book, it becomes a bestseller overnight. Crash a plane, you survive. You get a neighbor you don't want—she turns out to be a widow with no children. Me? I can't even—" Looking positively sick with fear, he suddenly didn't seem to know where to look.

"Relax, Roger," Zach soothed, wishing his visitor hadn't been quite so successful at checking himself. "I'm sure you'll get your…due."

Going from green to red, Roger muttered, "Let's play," and moved the pawn he'd fingered before forward by two squares. "I thought I'd try a strategy that won a Moscow tournament a few years ago."

Zach smiled coolly. "I can't wait."

Long after the lights went off at 11 Raven, he stood in the darkness and thought about her. It was one way to get his mind off his mistake. The only way.

It had been a difficult weekend, stressful and confusing. He'd barely been able to work, and he couldn't sleep. He wondered if he ever would again.

Something had gone wrong. He hadn't meant to do what had happened. It wasn't his fault. He'd been expecting Judith...*Judith,* wanting to tell her he wouldn't go through with it. *She'd* been there instead. The one. He'd had no choice.

If only she hadn't resisted, then she wouldn't have suffered so. He would have done what he had to do, what she should have enjoyed. It *wasn't* his fault! But she'd been too suspicious. Worst of all, there had been no release.

Would Willa make that mistake? He had to warn her not to when her time came.

From his pocket he drew out the handful of silk and stealthily approached her house.

CHAPTER SEVEN

She was midway down the stairs Monday morning when the sound of squealing brakes, shouts and screams had Willa rushing the rest of the way. A glance out the living room window told her the commotion was coming from next door, and she hurried to the dining room window, where to her amazement a police car, as well as a sleek white convertible were parked in the front of Zachary Denton's house. Two men, one in uniform, were grappling with a hysterical woman.

"Monster! You're finished now! This time you've gone too far!" she screamed toward the house.

The sound carried easily through the storm windows. But what really shocked Willa was that she recognized the woman as a customer. Judith Somebody. Not one of her fav—

"Oh my goodness!"

It finally hit her. The woman's last name was Denton. *That* was Zachary Denton's ex-wife!

She'd never cared for the woman because of her pretenses and attitude, not to mention her tendency to pass hot checks. When she came into the store, Willa slipped back to her office as often as possible to avoid waiting on her. But she'd never considered the significance in the names. After all, Denton wasn't that uncommon. Texas even had a college town using it.

Her guess had been that Judith Denton was the wife of some Houston oil executive or real estate wheeler-dealer. However, now that she knew the connection, she still couldn't believe it.

What on earth was going on over there? Too curious to resist, she decided her morning coffee could wait and headed for the front door. At least she'd dressed better this morning. In anticipation of the movers who she needed to meet across town in a matter of hours, she wore jeans and one of A.J.'s shirts over a loose salmon-colored T-shirt. Covered from neck to ankle as she was, this time there was no way she could give out unwanted messages, she thought, opening the front door.

The splash of bright red against the white door was totally unexpected. She stared for several seconds before it registered that this was not good, not good at all.

Not again. Please, not again.

What was it this time? She hesitated in reaching for it, eyeing the thing—she thought it was a scarf, but if so, there wasn't much to it—between the knob and door as if it might sting or bite. Most important, though, she wondered who had put it there? When. *Why?*

Prompted by the continuing ruckus next door, she cautiously tugged the item free.

Her surprise deepened into shock. It wasn't a scarf, but a pair of women's lace-trimmed, bikini briefs. Not hers, but she recognized them just the same. She'd sold out of them at Whimsy for Valentine's Day.

"Open up, damn it! The police are here with me!"

The shrill voice snapped her out of her stupor. Crushing the silky material in her hand, Willa continued on her way next door. But her insides were quaking, her mind reeling because there was no way to accept, let alone convince herself that this latest *message,* and what was happening next door, was pure coincidence.

"Excuse me?" Willa carefully made her way through the two overgrown yards. "Mrs. Denton?"

Leaving the ex-Mrs. Denton to the suited man, the uniformed police officer stepped away from the over-excited woman he'd been trying to draw back from the stairs, and blocked Willa's path. "Who are you, ma'am?"

"Willa Whitney. I live next door—just moving in, actually—and I heard the commotion. I was wondering if I could be of some help."

Judith gave up her struggles with the other man, and focused on Willa. Her expression and tone were suddenly blank, almost trancelike, and her eyes...

Despite the warmth and humidity of the morning, Willa experienced a sudden chill. Judith Denton had blue eyes, and hair that though bleached nearly white, and cut extremely short in a spiky punk style, was still blond.

Oh, God, please let this be a dream. Let me wake up now.

"You..." Judith Denton murmured through barely moving lips. "You're moving in there? Don't. You'll be putting yourself in terrible danger. Don't *do* it!"

"All right, Mrs. Denton," the man in the already-limp and wrinkled business suit interjected. "You don't want to say anything that—"

"Don't call me that! Don't ever call me *Mrs.* Denton again!" Judith shrieked, turning on him like some wild thing.

"Why not? You went to all lengths to acquire the status."

Everyone turned to stare at the man who glared back at them with disgust. Willa didn't know how Zachary Denton had managed to open the front door without anyone hearing the bolt, but there he was on the other side of the screen door, looking fierce and untamed himself. Definitely ready to do battle. When his gaze settled on her, she had the strongest urge to hide behind the uniformed officer. "Arrest him!" Judith cried to the two men, as she pointed at her ex-husband.

Gently urging down her arm, the middle-aged man in the suit said, "Mr. Denton? I'm Detective Jack Pruitt, Vilary P.D. I'd like to ask you a few questions, sir."

"What for?" Zachary Denton demanded, making no attempt at civility.

"You monster, you know what for!" Judith shouted back. She wrenched free of the uniformed officer's hold and charged for the stairs again.

The uniformed officer, younger and more agile, especially since he wasn't wearing strapless red high-heeled sandals like Judith, reached her first. But the woman had no intention of being held, let alone calmed; she didn't even seem to care that her twists and lunges were parting the front of her matching red jumpsuit and offering quite a view of Whimsy by Willa merchandise. Blushing, the officer cast Willa a look of desperate appeal.

"Maybe you could help her, ma'am?" Detective Pruitt added, providing the unwelcome second to the motion.

Wishing she hadn't been so hasty in coming out here, Willa followed him up the stairs, and did what he'd asked, while the detective continued across the porch.

"May we come in, Mr. Denton?" Pruitt asked again, still painstakingly polite. "We really do need to discuss a few things."

"Only if you insist, Detective. But understand that I haven't had time to lock away my valuables. Therefore,

I'm holding you responsible for my ex-wife's behavior. She has a penchant for taking what's not hers."

"Bastard," Judith spat at him.

Willa didn't know whether to feel sorry or embarrassed. Although she already had experienced a taste of how rude Zachary Denton could be, she couldn't believe he would be so blatantly cruel in front of two strangers, let alone officers of the law. However, her objective study ended the instant she again found herself under his scrutiny.

"I see your experiences haven't left you any the wiser," he muttered to her as they filed into the house.

However disheveled, Zachary Denton looked confident and in control as he wheeled his chair back several yards. Willa understood quickly that it was so he could see them all at the same time—perfectly logical for a man who was an expert in providing surprises in his stories, but didn't like them happening to him.

"All right, what's this about?" he demanded, folding his massive arms across his chest.

"Don't pretend you don't know," Judith flung back at him. "You thought it was me you were getting, didn't you? Were you at least *sorry* when you realized it was Nancy instead?"

Sighing and combing his hands through the wild tangle of his hair, he glanced at Detective Pruitt. "What the hell is she talking about?"

If it was an act, Willa decided he belonged onstage. He appeared as confused about all this as she felt.

"Ms. Denton was out of town on a business trip this weekend," the detective began in the telling monotone of someone who preferred getting answers rather than being asked questions.

With a harsh laugh, Zachary Denton replied, "Business trip! Shame on you, Jude. Tell them it was your yearly vampire convention. Thanks to Anne Rice, you and your kind are all the fashion again.''

Detective Pruitt cleared his throat and gestured to Judith that he would handle the situation. ''This is a matter of great levity, Mr. Denton. Someone attacked the woman staying at Mrs. Denton's residence. Do you know Nancy Porter?''

''Unfortunately, although I try not to admit it in polite company. What do you mean, 'attacked'?'' Zachary Denton's implacable expression grew wary. Watchful.

The detective shifted and Willa received a brief glance. *He's uncomfortable, and he doesn't want to have to say this in front of me.* That could mean only one thing—it was bad. She wanted no part of it. ''I should leave,'' she offered, taking a small step toward the door.

''Stay!''

Both Zachary and Judith spoke in unison. The venomous looks that followed made Willa want to borrow from Solomon and quip, ''Sorry, guys, I'm fresh out of swords.'' She did, however, stay put.

''We're in the early stages of our investigation,'' Pruitt began again. ''Unfortunately, Ms. Porter is unable to assist us.''

''Are you saying she's dead?'' Zachary Denton asked, visibly tense.

Her hands clenched and shaking before her, Judith ground out, ''Stop pretending you don't know!''

In better moments, Willa thought, the woman would be considered attractive, definitely stylish. Her age was somewhere around forty Willa guessed, and when her nerves weren't shot, when her makeup wasn't smudged, and her eyes weren't bloodshot and tear-swollen, there would be a cool, intelligent sensuality that would turn many a head. But at the moment, she was all pain and venom.

"Mrs.—*Ms.* Denton," Detective Pruitt injected more firmly this time, "please let me handle this." A stolid man with the likable, but humorous face of a bullfrog, he eyed everyone from beneath heavy lids, finally redirecting his attention on Zachary Denton. "She's not dead. Ms. Porter has been taken to Vilary Pines Hospital. However, it's too early for a prognosis. There's evidence to suggest she'd been sexually assaulted and then strangled. Unfortunately, she's unconscious, and unable to tell us what she knows."

Zachary Denton shifted to grip the arms of his chair, but it was his only physical reaction. "That's...terrible news, and I'm sorry to hear it, but I'm afraid I don't know how this is supposed to have anything to do with me."

"Ms. Denton seems to believe—" Detective Pruitt's lips only thickened as he pressed them together. "Please excuse me if this question seems accusatory, sir, but can you prove your whereabouts over the last twenty-four hours?"

Zachary's bold features took on a devilish slant as he lifted an eyebrow. "Look at me, Detective. Where do you think I was? The local bowling alley?"

"It won't work, Zach," Judith said, her smile glacial. "I told him about the van in your garage that's adapted to get you anywhere you want to go."

Zach watched the shock in Willa's lovely eyes, watched it grow into unease and renewed doubt. It annoyed him as much as Judith's accusations did.

What had she expected? Did she think those ramps

out there were for him to practice wheelies during recess? So he had a van. Big deal. For the most part the thing stayed in the garage out back because he preferred to forego the pleasure of being stared at like some sideshow freak, and have everything he needed delivered.

But sometimes when the writing wouldn't come and the house was suffocating him, late, late at night when virtually everyone else was asleep and the streets were his, he took the van out for a spin down the back roads. Alone, except for the other nocturnal creatures, he challenged fate to stop him, to put an end to the rage and the fever of revenge that was all that kept him alive.

It never did, of course.

If he'd known it would only take that bit of knowledge, the admission of the van, to make Willa *really* fear him, he would have mentioned it sooner. But at least something had finally gotten through to her. At least he knew he would never have to deal with the temptation of her again.

Crossing his arms once more, he refocused on Judith and matched her smile for smile. ''Yes, I own a van. But no doubt *you've* tried to convince them that I rolled myself into my secret death chariot, and drove to your house hoping to find you there so I could finally be rid of your carnivorous presence in my life. How'd I do it, Jude? Did I wheel to the bottom of your steps and drag myself up your stairs? How did I ring the doorbell? Or did I just pound until someone answered? Your neighbors must have had quite a show. But, then, they're probably well bored by the diversity of what crawls up your driveway, and never bothered to look.''

Although livid, Judith spun to Detective Pruitt. ''Ask him how he knows there are steps to my front door. Ask him!''

Zach let his smile widen. "I have no problem telling you, Detective. I had photographs taken of her...*cottage*. Call me eccentric, but if I work like a dog, I'd like to at least have a clue as to where my money's gone." He turned back to his ex-wife, enjoying that she was beginning to resemble a swaying cobra. "But back to your story—what happened then, Jude? I supposedly attacked someone I thought was you?" He shook his head. "And you call *me* over the edge."

"You know damned well, you hired someone to do your dirty work, but they blew it!" she snapped back at him.

"Jude—"

"Stop calling me that!"

"*Jude,* the day I come after you, believe me, the last face you see will be mine."

Pruitt exchanged glances with the uniformed officer. "Mr. Denton, that will be enough."

Zach couldn't agree more. "Exactly why are you here, Detective? *Am* I being added to your list of potential suspects? If so, I believe I'd prefer to telephone my attorney first."

"I don't believe that will be necessary, but I'd feel more confident in saying that if you weren't so...''

"Verbal in my dislike for my ex-wife?" Zach beamed. "Sorry, Detective. She just brings out that side of me."

Pruitt cleared his throat and nodded to Judith. "I felt it was in the best interest of everyone that we follow Ms. Denton out here, and make sure that this already unfortunate situation doesn't expand to where there're more casualties. Having said that, and understanding perfectly that you owe me no explanation whatsoever, would you mind telling me your whereabouts over the last twenty-four hours?''

"Not at all. I was here."

"Can you prove it?"

Zach glanced at Willa, not surprised when she lowered sweeping lashes over her gem-bright eyes. "If I must. But I don't plan to until—"

"What's that?"

Judith had lost interest in him, but only because of Willa—or more accurately at what she was clutching in her hand and discreetly trying to tuck into the back pocket of her jeans. His ex-wife grabbed her wrist and tried to take it from her, clawing at it, at Willa, and making whimpering, almost animallike noises.

Both policemen rushed forward to stop her.

"Those are Nancy's!" Judith cried. "I mean they're mine, but Nancy was— Oh, don't you *see?* It matches the camisole she was wearing. It's a set. Ask *her.* I bought it at her store! Where did you find these?''

Judith finally gained possession. That's when Zach saw they were red ladies' briefs.

Horrified, but quickly snatching them back, Willa gasped, "Stop it! Mrs. Denton you've made a terrible mistake. These are mine. I own a set of practically everything I sell at my shop."

Zach studied the heightened color in Willa's cheeks, and the way she avoided Judith's gaze. But most of all he enjoyed that at least for the moment Judith had lost credibility with the two cops. "Nice try, Judas, Jr.," he drawled. "But no silver this time."

As expected, the second and ultimately insulting nickname he'd christened her with at the end of their marriage sent her ballistic. She charged at him like a madwoman.

"I hate you! I hate you! *I hate you!*"

He managed to swing his chair sideways and keep her from landing on top of him, but there was no fighting velocity. When she shoved, the chair went flying and so did he, crashing to the hardwood floor with a loud crack, and a blinding pain shooting through him.

"Mrs. Denton! Harper, get her out of here before we have two patients for Emergency!" Pruitt snapped before crossing to offer his aid to Zach. "You okay? Here, give me your hand."

Instead, Zach shut his eyes, knowing he had to wait for the dizziness, agony and rage to ease before he tried moving again. "Get out."

"Let me get you up first."

"*Out!*"

For several seconds, the only sound was Officer Harper leading out a violently protesting Judith. Then came Pruitt's indecipherable mutter and a heavy sigh.

"I'm sorry about this."

"Ask me if I care." Zach was preoccupied with wondering why he hadn't heard Willa leave, too.

"You do understand that I may have to come back?"

"Well, if you do, make sure you bring the appropriate paperwork, and leave *her* at home."

The older man didn't reply. A moment later Zach could hear him shuffle away. Pause. Then, "Can I see you to your house, Ms. Whitney?"

"In my case it's Mrs., Detective Pruitt. And, um, I think I'll…"

Zach hadn't been able to resist peeking, but as soon as he saw her gesturing toward him, he closed his eyes again. He didn't want to see what she was doing. If she chose to stay, then it was on her head.

"Are you sure you know what you're doing?"

Waiting for the answer, he didn't know what he felt more, the blood pounding at his temples, or the egg hatching from the back of his head.

"Yes. I'll be fine, thank you."

When the door slammed shut behind the cop, and his footsteps were no longer distiniguishable on the porch, Zach exhaled a long-pent-up breath. Opening his eyes, he looked directly at Willa, who hadn't budged an inch.

"Why did you lie?" he demanded.

CHAPTER EIGHT

Willa listened to the cars leaving. One made as much noise as when it arrived; the other almost sounded weary as it drove off.

"Are you saying Judith was right?" she countered to Zachary Denton. She was growing increasingly repulsed by the soft silk that felt like a brand against her skin. Wishing she'd never heard that, she began shoving the briefs into her pocket. "Are these hers? I mean, could her friend have been..."

"Wearing them?" With a vicious shove, he pushed the heavy chair off his thigh. "If you believe I know the answer to that, it makes you quite the fool for staying behind, doesn't it?"

She knew that. The truth was already as obvious as the humid air seeping through the screen door, and it added to the tension pulsating between them. But she still had to have her ultimate question answered.

As if reading her mind, Zachary Denton swore and eased himself up on one elbow. "All right...let's put it this way. No doubt red would be a striking on you, but if I were doing the choosing, I'd go with black, myself."

"I prefer white," she murmured, almost weak with relief.

His gaze swept downward, and he was all insolence. She knew he was recalling her outfit the first time she came here, but also letting her know the comment meant nothing. Nevertheless, Willa meant to hold fast to the small ground he'd yielded.

"Where did you find that?"

This question came reluctantly, too. She finished tucking the briefs into her back pocket. "On my front door."

"Why didn't you tell Pruitt?"

"I'm not sure."

"You don't lie well."

His subtle mockery, along with his penetrating gaze had her mouth feeling incredibly dry. She had to lick her lips to manage a reply. "Maybe I thought that somehow I was being used as a pawn, and resented it."

He narrowed his eyes. "The queen," he murmured, as though realizing something for the first time. "It would have to be the white queen."

Now he'd really lost her. "Excuse me?"

"Just theorizing."

Maybe so, but the barely leashed violence she saw in his dark eyes made Willa feel less than confident again. Hoping to reach the side of the man she'd glimpsed once, and all-too-briefly, she cautiously lifted the wheelchair upright. "You're not easy to read, Zachary Denton, let alone like. Maybe some of that's understandable considering what you've been through. Personally, though, I'm not sure I think it's an acceptable excuse for being an ass. But the bottom line is...as much as I've tried, as spooky as you can get, I don't think that what's going on around Vilary is your doing."

Even sprawled on the floor, he managed to convey a threat. "No? You can't picture me on my way home from attacking one of my ex's houseguests, and stopping at your place to present you with a souvenir of my adventure?"

"It sounds even more ludicrous when you suggest it. You may be capable of a great many things, Zachary, but I don't think rape is one of them."

It wasn't the strongest protest she'd ever made; nevertheless, it won her an annoyed snort, and the growl, "Set the damned brake, Florence Nightingale, unless you want to see me flopping around this floor like a beached whale again."

Wondering if his rudeness had anything to do with self-consciousness, she secured the lever he'd indicated. Then he surprised her by extending his hand.

"Would you mind?" he growled, when she hesitated.

It was like having a grizzly bear asking you for a hand into a picnic basket. Willa's first impulse was to doubt his motive, but she quickly reminded herself that she would be defaulting on the very message she'd been trying to give him. Bracing herself, she gave him her hand.

In the next bewildering moment, she found herself down on the floor with him. She'd landed hard across his chest, but except for a deep grunt, he seemed barely affected by the impact, while she was left gasping and once again wincing in pain from his merciless grip on her upper arms.

"Now tell me what you find ridiculous," he whispered, his gray eyes steely.

Aware of what was coming, she gasped, "Zach—don't! Not this—"

She wanted to rear back, but as if he'd anticipated it, he shifted one hand to wind it around her long ponytail, trapping her against him. Then he crushed his mouth to hers, forcing open her lips and driving his tongue deep into her mouth. Her hands were useless, crushed be-

tween their bodies, imprisoned there by the viselike arm
he secured around her back.

Panic peaked and surged like a dreaded tidal wave,
and she wondered if it was possible to suffocate on a
scream. This was nothing like before. No one had ever
exposed her to such violence. He might think he was
no longer the man he once was, but he still had the
ability to make a woman feel insignificant and vulnerable.

On the edge of terror, she reached deep, wrapped
herself in the memory of those few seconds from Friday
when she'd seen his concern for her, felt his torment
and loneliness…and his desire. Only then could she let
herself, force herself at first, to stop fighting him. To
relax.

He was slow to realize the surrender. When he did,
he, too, went still; then slowly he lowered his head to
the floor and stared up at her.

"Fight me," he demanded gruffly.

His invincible hold made it impossible for her to
shake her head without hurting herself. She tried anyway.

"Damn you!" he whispered.

For a moment she had the strongest feeling he would
shift his hold and wrap his hands around her throat, he
looked that provoked. Maddened. But to her amazement, instead he eased his grip on her hair…the band
around her back. Ever so slowly, he slid his hands to
frame her face, caressing as he coaxed her head down
until her lips were a breath away from his.

Their gazes locked in some silent duel of wills, he
rocked his head to brush his lips against hers
once…twice. Then he drew her lower lip between his
teeth and teased it with the tip of his tongue. He might

as well have triggered a switch. Her entire body became sensitized. She had no more control over the soft entreaty that rose up her throat, than she could keep her eyelids from drifting closed, or her lips from parting.

He sucked in a deep breath swelling his chest and lifting her. The movement, teased her breasts, and tightened the coil pulsating in her womb like a living needful thing. His tongue became another instrument of sensual torture, venturing, exploring, and this kiss was no assault by any stretch of the imagination, but a claiming nonetheless.

Now she understood a real reason to fight him, but as he explored and stroked, she could only yield and follow, coax him to do more. It had been too long since she'd felt this alive. So long. When he coursed a trail of kisses across her cheek and down her throat, she arched to give him easier access.

"Oh..."

His groaned whisper heated flesh already hot and straining, and this time when he sought her mouth, there was only craving, a hunger she'd never had to deal with before. Her own. How odd that instead of having to deal with his anger her punishment came in waiting for more of him.

He stroked the silkiness of her hair...tested the sleek, smooth line of her back...the narrowness of her waist...the curve of her bottom, around and up to the aching swell of her breasts. All the while he studied her, as if her emotional reactions were as important to him as the tangible physical ones.

The kiss that followed made her head swim and all but drew the air from her lungs. Slow, thorough, insatiable, it went on and on, an endless draining, until he tore his mouth from hers and abruptly rolled her onto her back.

He glared down at her. "No more."

His protest was more plea than demand, but either way she had no intention of arguing with him. It was crazy enough to have felt such intensity and recklessness. She shouldn't even be here; she was supposed to be on her way to her apartment to meet the movers for heaven's sake!

"And stop looking at me that way!"

"How? The way you're looking at me?"

"Hell…" He drew back, slumping back on the floor. "Just what do you think your clientele will think once they find out you've involved yourself with a man suspected of murder?" he demanded, gazing up at the ceiling.

"Involved myself…have I?"

"Not if I can help it."

The velvet and desire was gone from his voice, and the cold, cutting edge had returned. Back in character, he made her yearn over the loss of what she'd only glimpsed and tasted.

"There hasn't been a murder," she pointed out to him.

"Yet."

Willa sat up, determined to make her point. "Even if that poor woman dies, you can't convince me that you did it—or arranged for someone else to," she added, to counter another possible comment.

"Keep making a pest of yourself and I may decide to change your mind."

She watched him maneuver back into his chair. It was slow-going, and she wanted to help, but knew better than to try. Despite his injury, he managed well enough, moving with commendable control and strength.

When he was settled, she continued. "I'm merely asking for answers." Knowing she would need the height for confidence, she pushed herself to her feet. "If you don't tell me what's going on, I'm going to go ask Judith. It has something to do with her, doesn't it?"

"Stay away from her!" Zach roared, nearly coming out of his chair again.

Willa took a cautionary step backward, but challenged, "Give me a good reason why. Not *one*—a good one."

"I'll give you the only one that matters. This is none of your business!"

How could he say that? "Someone's making it my business! I've had an anonymous note put in my mailbox. Today, I've been given what may be an assaulted woman's underwear...."

"All the more reason to stay out of this."

He was unbelievable. "Has it occurred to you I'm not being given a choice?"

His face took on that strained, closed expression she was beginning to recognize. The one that said things between them were deteriorating rapidly.

"You would have been if you'd listened to me. If you'd kept away." Gripping the armrests of his chair, he leaned forward, his expression intense, his gaze hypnotic. "I told you that I don't like intruders, and nothing's changed. I *don't* want you."

Words meant to hurt, to repel. They succeeded somewhat, but Willa still stroked a finger over where his beard had burned her. "Yes, I noticed how much you don't. You should get your messages clear, Zach. It's a bit strange to kiss a woman the way you do, and then tell her it was nothing.''

''So call me strange. Others have accused me of worse.''

Enough was enough of this bizarre merry-go-round, she decided. She was even losing a grip on what *she* believed. ''If you say so,'' she murmured, turning toward the door.

''Willa.''

She stopped, aware of the tingling sensation that coursed through her body at the sound of her name on his lips, but she refused to turn around. ''What?''

He hesitated. ''You have beautiful skin. I'm sorry for hurting you.''

It wasn't much to grasp on to, but Willa did a slow pivot anyway. ''I'll heal. It wouldn't hurt *you* to shave, though.''

He looked as if she'd suggested the most outlandish thing. ''Why bother? It's a waste of time. Besides, this isn't likely to happen again, is it?''

''Who knows? There's no telling when I'll test your temper again.''

His head moved back as if he'd taken a clip on his sturdy chin. ''Have you always had such an adventurous spirit?''

''Actually, marriage slowed me down.'' The memories coaxed a sad smile. ''With A.J. being a rescue helicopter pilot, I thought someone in the family needed to keep their feet on solid ground.''

''I remember hearing about the crash. He was a fool for flying in impossible conditions.''

His criticism didn't upset her. She understood it was the pilot in him reacting, that's all; they were by experience, if not nature, an intensely safety-conscious species. "There were justifiable reasons," she told him, knowing he would understand. "The little boy he'd been trying to save had been severely injured in a tractor accident north of here. The child's only hope, small though it was, had been the specialists in Houston."

"Instead, everyone was lost."

She backtracked to his chair and crouched before him, knowing what he was driving at. "The crew was committed to what they believed in. If they had the chance to do it all over again, I know they would still have taken the risk. It took me a long time to accept that. You can't stop people from doing what, in their hearts, they know they have to do."

Was that a flicker of admiration she saw in his penetrating gaze? It wasn't what she'd set out to get from him. She wanted his trust. Just a few grains to start. Maybe she could help him. Heaven knows why she felt he needed it, or what she could do for that matter, but the pull was there.

"Do you play chess?"

Perplexed, she shook her head, giving him a quizzical frown.

"Maybe you should. You're quite the strategist."

"I'm not playing games."

His expression exposed his skepticism. "All of life is a game. Everything we are is geared toward maneuvering, jockeying for position, feints, threats." A flicker of desire flared again as he let his gaze roam over her features. "The trouble is that most people haven't a clue as to what they're doing."

"Is this a variation of the 'be careful for what you ask' lecture?"

"Take it seriously."

"You've made it impossible to do otherwise." Willa

touched his hand. "And I still intend to find out, so please, *you* tell me. What's going on around here, Zach?"

At first he didn't reply, and she wondered if he would. He kept staring at their hands, a frown building like summer thunderheads across his broad forehead.

Suddenly he pulled free and crossed his arms. "I told you. There's a stalker who's after blond, blue-eyed women."

"Is Nancy Porter a blue-eyed blonde?"

"She and Judith could be twins...in more ways than one."

Willa sorted through that answer, wishing that pieces of the puzzle weren't starting to fit so neatly. She didn't like the picture she was getting.

Finally she had to ask, "It's not a coincidence, is it?"

"So you're starting to put it together."

"You mean this does all tie in with her?" she whispered, aghast. "Judith really was the target?"

"What an appealing thought," Zach drawled, looking anything but apologetic for how that sounded. "However, no. I think he's out to make it *look* as if she is...and that *I'm* the one who's stalking her."

A puzzle inside a puzzle. Willa found such thinking, such scheming, more than outlandish, it was frightening. "How did you pick up on this?"

"I didn't."

"What do you mean?"

"You're not the only one to have heard from our friend. I've received notes from him, too."

CHAPTER NINE

This time Willa didn't try to assimilate the information. It went beyond anything she'd ever had to deal with before. "You? Why would he be sending you messages if he's trying to frame you?"

"Because he *is* a fan?"

Willa rose to stretch her legs and think about that. "I heard Stephen King had some problems awhile back with an overzealous admirer of his work. Is this a case of the darker the writer, the more twisted the fan?"

"I wouldn't know. This is my first."

If he was trying to console her, he'd failed.

"The point I'm making," Zach continued, "is that he knows me, knows my style, the way I try to construct my stories, how it's not enough for me to simply scare the hell out of my readers temporarily, but permanently."

That much she understood. A.J. had once insisted on reading to her from *Snakecharmer,* and to this day she couldn't look at the most innocent tattoo without shuddering. "Are you saying he wants to compete with you?"

Zach's answering look held a shrug. "He's certainly presented me with one convoluted and challenging plot. And so far he's invited interaction by letting me try to solve the mystery, trusting that I'll figure out a way to keep the law off my back while he keeps pointing them in my direction."

"That's insane, not to mention sadistic. He'd have to despise you to do such a thing."

"Would he?"

Seeing his brief, bitter smile, she gaped. "He certainly can't expect you to reward him?"

"I think he did. Once. But not lately. Now I have an uneasy feeling that in the end I'm supposed to fail. Still, I'm not about to discount anything. The police won't."

"What do you think has made him change?"

"A taste for what he's doing." Zach shrugged.

Something about the dismissive move was too practiced. "You have another theory, though, don't you?"

He eyed her for another long moment. "He may not be working alone, and it could be he's fallen under the influence of someone less enamored with my...persona. Someone who loathes me enough to want to destroy me once and for all. Someone so determined that if they don't succeed one way, they're willing to try another."

The way he'd said "once and for all" gave Willa the shivers. "Whoever he is—or *they* are—this has certainly frightened your ex-wife to death."

The lines around Zach's mouth deepened. "You bought that performance?"

"Her friend was attacked in her own house! I'll admit I'm not Judith's greatest fan, but to have something so—"

"For your sake, make sure she remains simply a customer." At her wide-eyed glance, he gestured to the door. "You forget, it's wired for sound out there. There's a twin out back, and in the garage."

That look was coming back into his eyes, the secrets and the hidden emotions that created those disturbing shadows. "You're trying to frighten me again."

"You heard it yourself—a woman's been taken to the hospital. I damn well mean to frighten you."

"Then let me see the notes!" she pleaded urgently.

"No! The only reason I told you about them is to make you see this isn't a game. Now forget I ever mentioned them."

"Zachary, what if I want to help you?"

Swearing violently, he spun his chair away as if trying to escape the very sight of her. "Are you this reckless with all men who admit they're hot for you, or is this Pity the Cripple Day?"

She thought she'd already witnessed the extent of his coldness and cruelty, but he'd just proven her wrong. As Willa felt the barbs dig deep, she wondered how simple words could hurt so much worse than bumps and bruises and cuts? She hadn't cried, really cried, since burying A.J., but suddenly she was blinded by tears, and knew if she didn't get out, she was going to make a grand fool of herself.

Spinning around, she ran for the door. To her horror it slammed and locked just as she reached it.

"Let me out!" She beat at the solid wood with her fist. "Let me go!"

The door remained shut.

Beginning to hyperventilate, she pressed her forehead to the cool oak. *Come on, Willa. You're stronger than this, and you know what he's doing.*

She drew in a shaky, but deep breath, and slowly turned around to face him. He remained in the middle of the foyer, the remote control in his hand. She had no idea where he'd been hiding it, and didn't care. She had only one priority at the moment and that was that he understand her. Completely.

"I haven't been with another man since my husband

died. Until today it never crossed my mind to change that because what A.J. and I shared was fulfilling and special. For you to suggest what you did is beyond—"

"I know," he said heavily. With an elbow on an armrest, he hid his face in his hands. "And I apologize."

Unfortunately, words were his forte, leaving her to wonder what she should believe or disbelieve. "I don't want your apology. What I want is an explanation for why you deliberately hurt me."

Will was an incredible thing. It made everything else like brains and brawn insignificant. Manifested by passion, it had the power to devour virtually any resistance. Willa had momentarily forgotten that, and now prayed for just enough of it to keep her sanity.

"Willa…"

"The truth."

Zach sat up, his face drawn and gray. "Because you're unattainable."

"That's not what you suggested a moment ago. Try again."

"That's it!" he snapped. His eyes burned with his own passion. "You think you needed to explain about your marriage? A man only has to look into your eyes to know who you are and what you've lost. You're not very good at hiding your emotions.

"But what you are good at is reminding me of all the ways I've failed." He briefly shut his eyes. "Looking at you forces me to face how happiness has evaded me, the peace I've lost, the faith I've never had. And—Hell, this is nuts."

"*Tell* me."

He turned his face away. "I hate knowing that even if I wasn't who I am, or how I am, you'd remain unattainable because no one can compete with your dead husband. Most of all, I hate being tempted to try anyway.''

Willa stared at his profile, wondering why she'd invited this; she was in no condition to deal with it, or him. He'd said it himself: not even Zach Denton was coping very well with Zachary Denton these days. And yet she heard herself murmur, ''Oh my God. You're afraid of feeling.''

''Feeling?'' His laugh was raw with pain. ''Honey, I'm afraid, period. I have been all my life. It was my earliest memory, and it's there in every minute of every day. It's like having a Siamese twin attached at the jugular. Why do you think I write what I do? Who else is qualified to jerk everyone's chain, but someone who's constantly dangling from the end of his own?''

Abruptly he pointed the remote control toward the door and released the latch. As it swung open Willa was nudged forward a few steps.

''Go on. Run. I won't bother you again. Take what's in your pocket and give it to Pruitt. Blame me for having made you lie about it. Tell him to come see me. Tell him anything you want, or don't tell him anything. Only, go.''

''You don't want me to.''

''The hell I don't.''

''Try the truth again, Zach.''

He wheeled toward her, stopping only when he was within touching distance. Then he closed his fingers around the two front tails of her overshirt and drew her closer, until she had to grab both armrests to balance herself.

''More than not wanting to want you,'' he murmured, his breath caressing her lips, ''I don't want you to get hurt. And you will if you don't stay away from me. He knows you're becoming my weakness. I don't know how, but he knows. It has to stop.''

Willa wondered if he could hear her heart pounding. "It's out of our hands. I'm meeting the movers shortly. We're stuck with each other. Your only option is to at least tell me who I should be most careful around. Who do you suspect?'' she asked, amazed that she could speak at all. Maybe it was because his eyes had lost their fever and wildness again. Maybe it was because, as unready as she was to deal with the sexuality between them, it was easier than his anger or his self-destructiveness.

Zach let go of her shirt and stroked her cheek with his right thumb where his whiskers had burned her. "You're the most— All right. But before I tell you, there's one more thing. If you do go to Pruitt, he'll interrogate the people I'm about to name. When he does, something more terrible than Nancy Porter will happen. Don't doubt it. It's been promised. Be certain you can deal with having that on your conscience.''

He'd been threatened through those mysterious notes he'd mentioned. So that was why he's been remaining closed-mouthed about what he knew, she thought, grateful that he'd finally shared that, but horrified, too. How had he coped this long with the weighty responsibility? She couldn't imagine holding the fate of some unknown person or persons in her hands, while having to withhold information from authorities! Suddenly she realized she no longer questioned whether he was losing his mind, she was wondering how he'd managed to keep his sanity for as long as he had.

"Zach,'' she whispered, aching for him. "It's been a nightmare for you, hasn't it?''

He didn't respond right away, and it was clear he still wanted to fight her. "I get by."

"How?"

"I think about doing things." The thumb that had been stroking her jaw shifted to glide across her lower lip. "Like this."

Her breath caught in her throat. Every nerve ending in her body had somehow altered to begin and end at her lips. Willa felt his caress in her breasts, in her womb…it even left her tingling down to her toes.

"Zach, maybe we'd better—"

Before she could finish, he did it again, and instinctively, her head followed the path of his thumb. She parted her lips at his slightest probing, and captured him lightly with her teeth, stroked him with her tongue.

Zach stiffened and desire flared in his eyes, but he also drew away. "Woman," he murmured, his voice thick, "I have a feeling you'd tempt a saint, and I've never been close to one."

She doubted that he'd meant to remind her of that first message from the stalker, but he did. "I didn't mean to—" She stepped back and shook her head. "This is crazy." She'd never fallen under such an erotic spell before. Passion, yes, she'd known her share, but to not be able to stop yourself…?

Zach apparently agreed and put a few more feet between them, then raked his fingers through the tangle of his hair.

"I'll tell you and then you'll leave, okay?"

"Yes. Good idea."

He nodded, looking almost relieved. "There are only three people who have regular and relatively easy access to this house, to accomplish what's going on. Unfortunately, all three of them have been acting strange lately, so pinpointing a chief suspect has been difficult.''

"Do you know why they're behaving that way? Do they know each other?'' When he frowned, she lifted one shoulder. "The stalker might think you're on to him and be playacting in order not to stick out.''

"Or as I said before, maybe he's been coached by someone else.''

Maybe, but could a person keep up such a pretense? At least she already knew the first of the three. "One is Ger Sacks. You were warning me the other day, though at the time I thought you were protecting yourself.''

"Then and now.''

Not quite sure what he meant by that, Willa said more quietly, "Who are the other two?''

"Roger Elias and Felix Fraser.''

She couldn't have been more doubtful than if he'd named her kindergarten teacher. "That's almost too bizarre to contemplate. Not the same Roger Elias who's the store manager at Lavender's?''

"He's also an aspiring writer. We play chess twice a week, and in return for help with my game, I critique his writing. He was the one person who was here late enough to deliver what's in your pocket. Most interesting is his face is scraped raw. From a fall, he says, and he didn't offer much more of an explanation, but he remained edgy throughout the evening. The interesting thing is that it could have been self-inflicted to hide fingernail marks.''

Willa wondered how she could find out if anything had been found under Nancy Porter's nails. But another thought seemed to cancel out the need.

"Wait a minute, that was last night. Judith said she found her friend this morning."

"Which means nothing. That so-called friend could have been lying there for hours. A whole day. It just suited Judith's purpose to insinuate otherwise."

The mere idea that the poor Nancy Porter might have been conscious for a little while, helpless and terrified, had Willa swallowing in revulsion for the heinous crime. "Why would your ex-wife lie about the time?"

"You heard her. Judith is determined to make people believe the attacker was me—or someone I'd hired with the intent of getting rid of her."

And that couldn't be the case because then the stalker would have realized he had the wrong woman. "I understand you didn't have a friendly divorce, but does she think you hate her so much that you would kill her?"

"She doesn't have to think. I told her myself."

The air conditioner shut off, leaving the house unnaturally silent for several seconds. It magnified the fact that Willa didn't know what to say.

"Ah...I've shocked you yet again," he murmured, watching her closely.

"Somewhat. I was lucky to have married my first love. My parents were childhood sweethearts. My sister married the boy she met on her first day at college. I don't understand how relationships that have been that close can deteriorate to what you're suggesting."

"Well, they say that there's a fine line between love and hate." His bitter smile returned. "But in my case, it's closer to the truth to say that the only thing my wife ever loved about me was my money. When I discovered that settling for a fraction of it in a divorce court wouldn't satisfy her, I felt justified in voicing my opinion of her right to live to a ripe old age.''

"I see. And when was this?"

"When I woke from surgery after she sabotaged my plane.''

Reviewers hadn't dubbed him the Crown Prince of Darkness for nothing, but even this was beyond dark. This was *sick*. "You think Judith...?"

"I know it. It was my plane. I'd checked it over thoroughly in preflight for a trip to Denver where I was scheduled to give a seminar. In the last minute Judith ran out of the office to tell me I had a phone call. She had a cup in her hand, but I didn't think anything of it. She's addicted to diet soft drinks, and it never struck me that she might just have ice water in it. That part of the airport was quiet that day. It was easy for her to circle to the fuel nozzle on the wing, which was low on that plane, unscrew it, pour in the water.''

He told his story dispassionately, but Willa thought that made it even spookier. "The plane could still fly?"

"High enough to make coming down deadly. I fought it the whole way, looking for a field to land in. At one point I thought I'd made it, too. Then I hit a hole and the plane flipped twice. To this day, I don't know whether I was thrown free or crawled.''

"Didn't the FAA find anything in their investigation?" Willa asked, thinking about how this must have compounded his fear.

"The plane exploded. Besides, Judith put on the performance of her life to make everyone believe her poor husband had gone over the edge and had become a raving lunatic.'' He gestured as if to say it was all a moot point. "I did the only thing I could—I filed for a divorce. You know what my devoted wife did? She hired the great white shark of lawyers. Today she's *still* sucking her fifty percent out of me. She will until the books I wrote during our marriage cease to yield any return."

Was that reason enough to commit murder?

"Through the centuries people have killed for the change in someone's pocket, the shirt on someone's back," Zach said, watching her, "and when I divorced her, although Judith gained a great deal, she lost more. You don't think the woman feels scorned?"

He laid it out so neatly, there was no missing what he meant. "You think Judith knows the stalker!"

CHAPTER TEN

"She more than knows him," Zach replied without inflection. "I think she's controlling him."

That was incomprehensible to Willa. "When? How? Good grief, Zach, he tried to kill her and put her friend in the hospital instead!"

"What if he got the right woman? What if Nancy was the target all the time? A sacrifice?" Before Willa could protest, he added, "I told you there's been a focus shift in the messages. Now it's as if two people created them."

Although she knew she sounded petulant, Willa muttered, "Well, I'm not likely to agree or disagree because you won't let me see them."

"And no amount of wheedling will change my mind."

Seeing that was true, she decided to determine a few things another way. "Do you realize what you're suggesting? You're saying Judith was capable of stopping a man who wanted to punish her in your behalf, maybe even kill her, and turned him into a robot who does whatever she wants! Then you suggest Roger Elias as one of the suspects? The man isn't exactly threatening," Willa said.

Zach remained indifferent. "What he lacks in size, he makes up for in passion. His emotions run quite deep."

Not as far as Willa was concerned. She'd seen Roger Elias at mall-management meetings. Not once had he voiced any dissent to their lessee on an issue, let alone challenged any decision. But when she said as much to Zach, he remained convinced.

"You've seen the chameleon in dress uniform. There's another side to clever Roger. The manipulator, for instance. He plays chess with a true warrior's spirit. You can't play well without it. Add that to a certain sexual frustration and you have a walking, breathing time bomb on your hands."

At least Ger Sacks had the muscle. He didn't, however, strike Willa as the kind of person who could have thought up anything so diabolical. "What was the other name you mentioned?"

"You don't know him. Felix Fraser, my agent."

"You suspect the man you're supposed to trust the most? And what's his motive supposed to be?"

"The other fifty percent of my estate. Everything that isn't signed over to Judith, or held in trust for my old school. Why not?" he added, as though she'd made some protest. "I have no family, no children. What's more, I've never really cared much about money or possessions. And I did put him through hell by marrying Judith. He'd warned me about her, but I didn't listen."

She didn't want to think about what Judith had done or said to muddle his mind so. Instead, she thought about how empty Zach's life sounded, how lonely. "But is Felix Fraser capable of turning on you? Is he capable of murder?"

"I happen to believe that under the right circumstances, everyone is capable of doing both."

Living alone out here, she wasn't surprised. "What's he like?"

"Someone who's stepped out of a time machine. The Medicis would have loved him. He's in his early fifties, tall, dark, but going gray...an elegant man who's extremely cerebral and disciplined.''

"That doesn't sound like someone who should be suspected of going off the deep end or trying to frame you," Willa warned gently. She couldn't help being doubtful.

"The other day, the night before you got your first message, he told me it would have been better if I'd died in that crash."

The room went completely dark and spun several times before Willa managed to take enough deep breaths to stop it. "Oh, God. I'm so sorry. Why did he do it?"

"Maybe because he was thinking about old business. You see he'd been the one on the phone the day I crashed."

"You're really scaring me now."

Jarred out of her brooding, Willa swung around to find Starla with arms crossed and foot tapping, making an earnest attempt at giving her the evil eye. However, at best her sunny-natured assistant managed to look confused and concerned.

"Oh, no. Did I miss something?" It was Thursday, her third day back after moving, and she was doing her best to concentrate and not let on that she had trouble keeping focused for even two minutes at a time. She'd thought revamping their window display would do the trick, but apparently Starla had noticed something was off anyway.

"You could say that." The younger woman fingered the Etruscan-style hoop in her left ear. "You only ignored our mailman, who you know dotes on you, and you directed your fussiest customer to check out the sale rack.''

Willa was glad for the sturdy wall behind her. It proved a reliable support as she dropped back her head and silently moaned her regret and embarrassment. Timothy, their mail carrier, was a sweetheart, only months away from retiring, and painfully shy. As for Mrs. Potter…well, the less she thought about how she was going to have to appease the wife of the chamber of commerce's current president, the better.

"Point me in the direction of the stockroom and I'll go lock myself in."

Instead, Starla eased the basket of silk violets from Willa's grasp, placed them before the lavender-and-plum negligee Willa had draped across a vanity chair and drew her back into the interior of the store. At least it was a quiet moment before the lunch hour. Willa noted that there were only two customers in the store, and they were involved in some enthusiastic gift-purchase conference.

"You're not getting off so easy." Starla drew her toward the checkout counter. "I've been biting my tongue ever since Tuesday when you came back here looking like a deer in someone's crosshairs. Now, enough's enough. I saw the article in the paper about Nancy Porter. I read Judith Denton's statement. Nowhere was there any mention of what happened to you. No, don't say it. You didn't tell anyone about the note, did you?''

Willa didn't bother denying it. The sooner her assistant satisfied her curiosity, the sooner they could drop the subject. "No."

"Why not?" Starla cried. "You said yourself that

he'd probably sent it. Add that to what Mrs. Denton says about him—''

"That doesn't mean it's the truth. The police haven't said anything, have they?"

"But the implications!"

"Forget it, Starla!"

Her assistant's expression turned wounded. "I only thought that maybe the police could get some fingerprints off it or something," she said quietly.

Indeed they could. Hers and Zach's. "Maybe so, but that's not going to happen because I don't have it anymore." Seeing no way to avoid an explanation, she made her friend vow to keep this between them, and then shared an abbreviated version of what had happened—minus Zach's disclosure of his list of suspects, of course. And all the while she tried to underplay the sexual tension between her and Zach as much as possible. It didn't fool her friend for one second.

"Wow," Starla said, whispering because the two customers had just passed on their way to the next section of the store. "Imagine if you told me the good stuff. It would be better than the movies. I know," she added with a grimace, "it's an awful thing to say, considering that poor woman's still in a coma. But the rest of it—you have to admit it makes a sizzling story."

Willa's face grew warm, as she remembered. *Sizzling* didn't cover it, or the restless nights she'd been having since as she relived the moments when Zach had reduced her to a creature of sensation.

"What did you do with the, er, new evidence?"

"Put them in a freezer bag and out of sight." And prayed that the panties had been stolen from a drawer and that she wasn't hampering the investigation.

"How long do you think it'll be before the police get

a warrant and search Zach Denton's house? No telling what else they'll find there. Maybe he even has some poor soul locked in his cellar or something.''

Starla's focus was changing almost as often as Willa's conclusions regarding the suspects. ''Will you stop! If I can see that he's not a likely suspect, why can't you?''

''Because I wasn't lucky enough to end up in his arms, so I'm thinking with a clear head,'' she drawled, only to sober again. ''Aren't you worried that Judith may be right about him?''

Willa arched her left eyebrow. ''We're talking about the Judith Denton who bounces checks here at least once a quarter and returns nearly half of what she buys.''

''Good point. Hey, you know what would be weird? What if she's making all those accusations because she's still in love with him and she's upset that he won't take her back? If she finds out what's happening between you two, I'd be worried about my own neck.''

''Will you stop! You're going from bad to worse.''

Willa snatched the mail up off the counter and sorted through it. But she couldn't deny being troubled that, for all the upheaval, the police were keeping their distance. Even when Detective Pruitt had returned Monday evening, stopping first at Zach's house, and then at hers, the subject never came up again. He'd been polite, almost conversational as he'd asked her questions. And although he'd taken out a pad and pen, he hadn't written down a thing. It had only been when he'd begun to leave that he'd let her know the visit was meant to be a subtle warning.

''Are you aware that Mr. Denton owes his wife a great deal of money, Mrs. Whitney?'' he'd asked, clicking his ballpoint pen over and over until it sounded like a ticking clock.

She'd had no idea what to say. "That isn't any of my business, Detective."

"During their divorce, Ms. Denton was able to convince the judge that she'd provided invaluable aid and support during her husband's recuperation and therapy, that it was only her enthusiasm and encouragement that made Mr. Denton complete the two un-finished projects he owed his publisher. As a result, the court awarded her—aside from the rest of the settlement—a sizable percentage of all income he may enjoy up to and including those two projects. Not surprisingly, Mr. Denton protested. Forcefully. He's also made it extremely difficult for her to collect, and I understand those two books have enjoyed an unparalleled success. He was even overheard threatening that he would see her in hell before he let her suck another drop of his blood."

"What does all that have to do with me, Detective Pruitt?" Willa had asked, recalling the comment Zach had made to Judith about vampires.

"You seem like a nice lady. I'd hate to see you get taken in by a man who might seem...vulnerable, but who may be quite unbalanced." His smile had been sympathetic, and about as authentic as the silk plants she had scattered around the shop....

Starla's voice brought Willa back to the present. "Let me have that."

Realizing her assistant was tugging the mail out of her hands, Willa struggled to catch up on what she might have missed. "What now?"

"Oh, nothing except that you just tossed out an invoice from your biggest supplier."

Fortunately, Willa didn't have to make any response

since their shoppers were ready to check out. Tongue in cheek, Starla suggested *she* ring up the purchases, while Willa gift-wrapped them.

Once the two women left, Starla spun around. "You know what you need? Something to release all this built-up tension."

"One crack about my love life and I'm leaving," Willa warned, her eyes narrowed.

"Actually, I was thinking about mine...and a way you can help yourself while giving me moral support. Let's join up next door."

They'd talked about it before, but Willa had always backed out, her schedule full, her concern about losing weight nil. Having just moved, she had even less free time in her schedule than before. "I don't know." She sighed, hating to have to disappoint Starla. She knew Starla desperately wanted to take care of those few extra pounds once and for all, but this was exactly what Zach had warned her about.

"Please? You're not going to believe who actually walked me into the mall yesterday and suggested I try a trial membership."

"Ger Sacks," Willa murmured, knowing that canceled any warnings she might have honored about being sensible.

"He was so sweet and rather shy behind that golden-boy smile. I wish someone like that would ask me out."

But Zach believed he might be capable of terrifying a woman. Maybe even murdering her. "Really?"

"Yeah, but you know the kind of guy I attract? What's-his-name over at Lavender's."

Was this a nightmare or what? "You mean Roger Elias?"

"No, the guy in the shoe department. What a creep."

Starla tapped a long fingernail tinted in an exotic bronze on the glass countertop. "I'm telling you a girl can't be too careful. I went there last night looking for a pair of pumps to go with that new leopard print dress I bought. He *accidentally* brushed his hand against my you-know-what...and then had the nerve to invite me for a drink. The guy has a potbelly worse than my father's, and I could use the top of his head as a makeup mirror!"

No sooner had she sighed with relief that Starla hadn't meant Roger Elias than Willa was disturbed by this latest revelation. "Wait a minute. Are you saying it would be acceptable if a more handsome man took a free grope?"

"No, of course not."

"And I suppose the poor guy is to blame for his receding hairline?"

Starla swept her golden-brown hair behind one ear and shot her a wry smile. "Okay, Mother Teresa, why don't you heap on the guilt a bit thicker. Is it so awful to want to be happy? Look at me! I'm reasonably attractive, I practice good hygiene."

Unable to hold back a smile, Willa hugged the younger woman. "You're lovely, bright, giving...and you're trying too hard. It's like couples who get all panicky because they've been working overtime to conceive a baby, only it's not happening."

"Oh, great. Now I'm neurotic."

"Stop it!" Laughing outright, Willa pushed her friend to arm's distance and gently shook her. "What do I have to say to get you to quit doing this to yourself?"

"Come with me to the club," Starla pleaded without missing a beat.

"I'm not feeling *that* sorry for you," Willa replied,

going back to the mail. Her smile grew wistful as she discovered a postcard from her parents. It was from Paris, and the picture was of the Louvre. She sighed. Tonight she needed to phone Kelly and see if she'd received one, too. It had been days since they'd talked. This whole situation was making her neglect what was important to her.

"Just for a week—the duration of the trial membership. Then I'll know if I'm making any progress or not." Starla followed Willa to the office in the back of the store.

With her weight or with Ger Sacks? As Willa put the bills and postcard on her office desk, the possible answers worried her. But what if Zach was wrong about Ger? Good grief, wasn't she taking a risk in giving her mysterious neighbor the benefit of the doubt?

If she accompanied Starla, at least she would have an opportunity to get to know Ger better, too. Then she could decide for herself what he was and wasn't capable of doing. Sound logic, she decided, shutting the door again. After all, she would never forgive herself if something happened to Starla.

"You realize you'll owe me big-time if I say yes?" she teased, eyeing the woman who stood practically holding her breath.

Starla let out a squeal and hugged her. "You won't regret this!"

"I hope so, hon." Over her shoulder Willa saw their reflection in the antique mirror by the robes. Starla had never looked prettier, or more excited. So why did that leave her with such a feeling of impending failure? "I'll try not to disappoint you."

CHAPTER ELEVEN

"**I** know you're disappointed in me, Zach, but put that thing down. I've apologized twice for what I said last week. What more do you want?"

Eyeing his agent through the open bore of the revolver he'd been cleaning, Zach murmured, "Stop squirming, Felix. It's not as if this is loaded. Yet." He did, however, lower the handgun...but only to slip the silver-cased bullets into the six chambers. It was Friday and barely noon. Too early for Felix.

"In my next life I'm not going to represent anything but women's fiction writers," Felix muttered, stepping out of aim.

Zach snorted. "There's a gesture. They already own the largest chunk of the market as it is."

"Who are you to complain? I can think of only three writers, who may equal or better the deals than you get."

Zach couldn't have asked for a neater opening. But then, that's why he'd made the comment in the first place. "Sure," he muttered, "but how many of them have financial sponges as ex-wives?"

"You were warned."

"Mmm...and aren't you glad I don't revere the ancient ritual of silencing the messenger?"

Felix looked thoroughly disgusted with him. "I'm glad to see you're in your usual positive mood."

"It's a strain, but I live not to disappoint." Zach nodded across the room. "Help yourself to the bar if my goodwill is becoming too much for you, and tell me what brings you out here? You usually call first,'' he continued, not minding at all that he'd added the subtle rebuke. ''Do we have business to discuss that I didn't know about?'' Unless there was something he had to sign, they could have done that over the phone.

''I was in the neighborhood and thought I'd drop this copy off.'' Felix drew an envelope from his slim valise and placed it on the desk before detouring for the bar. ''It's a memo to Carstairs about your need to postpone *Under the City* and present *Checkmate* first.''

''I thought you two discussed that over the phone the other day.''

''We did, but you'll remember that I also told you how disturbed he was by this deviation. You know the rumors about your, er, fragile mental state. This simply puts into writing your assurances that he's getting a project you're too excited about to delay. By the way, it wouldn't hurt to drop him a short synopsis as soon as you can to give him and the marketing people something to work with.''

''Uh-huh. Now what's the real reason you're up here?'' Zach couldn't argue about the memo; hell, he paid Felix to keep him out of hot water. But what bothered him was that it could have been faxed or express mailed, he thought, watching his agent hesitate adding red vermouth to the ice in the crystal tumbler.

''Why do you insist on making me upset you?''

''So my Judith antenna wasn't malfunctioning.''

Felix proceeded with the pouring. ''You know I owe her an accounting and check from your last royalty statement,'' he replied, sounding as weary as Sisyphus. ''Since I'm close to two weeks late, I thought I'd soothe her ruffled feathers by presenting it in person.''

Zach snapped the cylinder in place. "By all means, let's make sure she isn't insulted or inconvenienced." Furious, he jerked open the top drawer of his desk and laid the gun inside. "How much is she getting this time?"

"You know the percentage. You saw the statement."

Bitterness rose in him like bile, and he swore with renewed fervor. "Between you two and the IRS, I should be an artesian well!"

"What's done is done, Zach. Let's just work at keeping her out of our hair, shall we?"

Zach reached for his Scotch thinking that he would stop protesting the court's decision right after Judith was locked away for the rest of her miserable, conniving life. "Tell me, are you as afraid of her as you act, Felix?"

To his credit, his agent at least looked sympathetic, if not comfortable, as he crossed over to him. "I'm merely following the letter of the law." Taking a sip of his drink, he sat down in the armchair facing the desk. "By the way, I approve of this change in your appearance. You were even beginning to frighten me."

Zach wasn't in the mood for olive branches; but he knew that if he remained in his current caustic mood for much longer, his agent would run and an opportunity would be wasted. Zach grimaced at the thought and rubbed his freshly shaved face, his trimmed nape. He still needed a professional cut, but he'd removed the beard, mustache and some of his overlong hair this morning after a disturbing nightmare. He'd dreamed he'd been making love to Willa, but everywhere he'd kissed her, she'd begun to bleed.

"Well, we can't have that, can we?" he replied, smiling across the desk at the other man.

After only the slightest frown, Felix sat back and conscientiously tugging at the knees of his gray suit trousers, he crossed his long legs. "How's *Checkmate* coming along now? Have you worked out the plot any further?"

"Quite a bit, actually. In fact, I've been looking forward to running it past you. My protagonist's a writer who's being set up to take the fall for something hideous going on in this cozy, picture-book community—I won't bore you with the details, but suffice it to say there's sufficient gore to entertain my more bloodthirsty readers. And as if that wasn't enough, he trips over a clue that suggests he's being financially ripped off by this associate."

"Ripped off..."

"Yes, indeed. Now being the chess aficionado he is, he decides what the hell, he'll probably die stopping the psychotics trying to frame him, he might as well see if he can't set up the so-called friend, too."

"Set up to do what?"

Zach tilted his head and, hoping he displayed more amusement than pleasure, murmured, "Good grief, Felix, you must like the idea. You're suddenly as pale as your shirt."

"It's a fascinating plot," his agent replied awkwardly. "But—set him up to do what, Zach?"

"Why to make a fatal mistake, of course. Didn't I mention that at heart my protagonist's quite the radical in a dark sort of way? He wants his pound of flesh, and one way or another he means to get it." Chuckling softly, Zach raised his drink to the man staring at him, thinking, *if that isn't a look of unholy dread, I don't know my horror.*

* * *

"Having a good time yet?"

At the sound of Ger Sacks's voice, the hairs at Willa's nape—that should have been too weighed down with sweat to move—lifted. But casting what she hoped passed for a doleful glance at the man watching her form on the stair-climbing machine, she sought the energy and the oxygen to reply. "Great. Terrific. Can't think of anything…else…I'd rather be…doing."

His grin deepened. "You're looking good, Mrs. Whitney. Especially for a first-timer. Real good."

"Are my hands positioned right, Ger?"

Starla's query came quickly, and maybe a tad too sharply for Willa to think it was anything less than frustration. It made her want to jump off her machine, tug her friend off hers and head for the nearest exit. She had that bad a feeling about what was happening.

But as if to make her think she was imagining things, Ger immediately circled over to shift Starla's hold back a few inches on the U-shaped bar. "There. That's it. This way you're not leaning forward as much and putting excessive strain on the small of your back. You want to use the whole leg. Watch Mrs. Whitney. Her form's perfect."

"It always is," Starla muttered, staring straight ahead.

Willa decided she'd had enough. "I don't know how you can keep up the pace and still look so fresh, Starla. I'm going to call it quits before I end up too sore to walk tomorrow."

She dismounted and used the towel around her neck to dab at her throat and forehead, wishing she hadn't given in to Starla's request. It had been a mistake to pick up the leotards and tights, to come here at all. She certainly wasn't going to come here again. She hadn't gained any useful information regarding Ger Sacks.

"Fine with me." Starla got off her machine, as well, and tugged at her leotard. "But you should have said something sooner. It was silly that you needed to turn this into an iron-man competition your first time out."

Incredulous, and more than a little exasperated, Willa watched Starla head for the women's changing area. She couldn't believe what she'd just heard.

"I hope she wasn't upset about something I said," Ger said.

"Well, it's a little late to worry about that isn't it?" Willa replied.

A troubled frown barely marred Ger's handsome face. "'Scuse me? I was only trying to explain we don't get into competition here. Man, if she took something—*anything*—I'd said the wrong way...well, I could get into trouble, Mrs. Whitney."

Was she losing her mind? Willa studied the soft-spoken giant. He sounded truly apologetic, as well as completely oblivious to what he'd done.

Bewildered, she shook her head. "Would you excuse me? It really has been a long day, and I think it's time for both of us to be getting home."

"Sure, I understand. But, um...do you like what you've seen?" When she blinked at him, he gestured around the facilities. "Do you think you'd like to extend your trial membership? I don't mean to push," he added, again the shy grin surfacing. "But with every membership we bring in we earn points toward a vacation in Hawaii."

"I see." But she didn't care for hard sells, even if it came more from management than from the man. "Let me sleep on it, all right?"

"You bet. Sweet dreams."

This time the tingling spread all the way up and down her spine. It was all Willa could do not to run for the lounge. Between Zach's spooky suppositions and the stalker's notoriety, her nerves were going fast.

She found Starla collecting her things, a stormy set to her flushed face. Sighing inwardly, Willa unlocked her rental locker. "What was that all about back there?"

"Please. I'm really not interested in doing this."

As the younger woman swung her purse strap over her shoulder and headed for the rear exit, Willa had to hurry not to be left behind. It was nearly ten o'clock and the parking lot was emptying fast. Fortunately she and Starla had parked close to one another and beneath one of the tall security lights.

"Wait a minute," she pleaded, once she caught up. "You're not interested in doing *what?* What happened in there?"

Starla wheeled around, her manner feverish, her look venomous. "You had to do it, didn't you? Your need for attention, to prove you're attractive and can have anyone you want made it irresistible."

The accusation couldn't have been more of a shock if it had come with a bucket of ice water. Willa looked up at the lights, at the traffic zooming past on the interstate and back at the health club where a bright white star flashed beside the name Vilary Vantage Health Club and Spa. No, she thought, this wasn't some bad dream; it was really happening.

"My *need* for attention? Starla, I don't deserve that, and if you'll think back, I wouldn't have gone there at all if it wasn't because you *asked* me."

"Oh, stop it, Willa! On top of everything else, I don't want to listen to you justifying yourself."

Since when did discussion and explanation become a negative? Willa shifted her belongings into the basket of one arm and held up her freed hand. "I think maybe we both need to cool off and do some rational thinking about this. Be careful going home, and I'll see you tomorrow."

Somehow she made it into her van. But by the time she was out of the parking lot and driving down the street toward home, she was shaking and the threat of tears made every muscle in her face hurt, her eyes burn. She fought for control, not wanting to give Starla's tantrum more power over her than necessary. But she wished she could understand.

What had happened? Starla had never behaved this way before. Suddenly Willa had found herself facing a total stranger, a stranger who'd removed the mask of friendship and goodwill and had glared at her with resentment, and jealousy—even hatred. What had triggered that? Was it Starla's growing confusion and frustration with the various machines, combined with her insecurity about her body—unjustified as well as inaccurate, as far as she was concerned—that triggered this, this irrational, emotional explosion?

What a relief to get home. At least the fiasco had managed to take her mind off her other concerns, she thought shaking her head. She killed the van's engine and eyed Zach's house. As usual, the only light seemed to be coming from his upstairs office.

They hadn't spoken since Monday. Moving in her possessions had eaten a great chunk of time, but she'd gone over Tuesday evening thinking she and Zach might compare notes regarding Detective Pruitt's visit; however, Zach hadn't let her in. Instead he'd keyed the audio on his sophisticated monitoring system and muttered, "Go home, Willa."

She'd gone, determined to give a new definition to space and privacy, angry that after exposing her to threat and danger, he would deprive her of any feedback or input. But just a glance at his broad back through the blue-net drapes, and she knew that wasn't the only reason for her ire. She resented him because with one glance he reminded her of what he'd made her feel. No matter how exhausted she tried to keep herself, just thinking of him could rouse inner cravings. Even now, tired and hurting, provocative sensations made her still-heated body oversensitive and damp.

"You're a glutton for punishment, pal."

Collecting her things, she backtracked to the mailbox, relieved to find only legitimate mail inside. Thanks to her set timer, the front porch light had been triggered at dusk, and she had no trouble unlocking the door.

Once inside, she exhaled with relief and pleasure, thinking she at least had this. How she was beginning to love the place. The first thing she saw was her favorite painting of an underwater scene of a school of fish, and on the long table beneath it were scattered shells, a crystal seahorse and a potted white azalea she planned to plant outside once it had finished blooming.

The rest of the room matched it for charm and romance. She'd sewn the floral covers for the ivory sofa and chairs herself, and the large ficus and rubber tree plants were like old friends, babied since moving into her first apartment after college. Even the coffee table had a story. A.J. had found the antique diving helmet on their honeymoon and they'd set it inside the huge glass-bowl base, adding driftwood and polished stones to make it look like the floor of the sea.

But tonight, neither the souvenirs of tender, happy times with A.J., nor the freshness that came with starting over, were enough to soothe the tension churning inside her. Unloading her armful of belongings onto the nearest chair, she headed for the kitchen. Almost past the dinette window, she froze…backtracked a step.

At first she thought she'd been seeing things. If it hadn't been for the chair, she would have thought it was someone else looking down at her through that upstairs window. But there he sat, for once the curtains pulled back, the computer light creating a nimbus of blue around him while some other illumination lit his face. That face, she realized, was clean-shaven, and very much like the intelligent, handsome man she'd seen on the inside cover of his novels.

Why had he done it?

She didn't need this. Not tonight.

He reached behind him for something…glanced down a moment, then lifted it to his ear. His phone. A moment later hers rang.

Her heart did a panicky flip-flop, and she told herself that Starla was calling to apologize. Maybe her sister. Oh, God, what if the baby was early?

She sprang for the phone. "Hello?"

"You're late tonight."

His voice, but she couldn't believe it. Once again she backtracked to look out the window.

"How did you get my number?"

"Far too easily. You should consider getting a private listing. You never know who could get hold of it."

He was right. "I may do that."

She waited for what would come next. Nothing did. He simply sat there watching her, and all she heard was his breathing.

"I almost didn't recognize you," she said, although she'd wanted to wait him out. "That's some close shave."

"Took me three throw-away razors to get it all off." He swept his hand over his hair. "Still need some work on the rest."

She couldn't resist. "Preparing for a new press photo?"

"Nothing so public," he replied, a wry smile in his voice. "More like an apology."

"Really? Who's the lucky soul?"

"My neighbor."

She wondered if he heard her heart trip all over itself on its race up her throat. "Any special reason?"

"Pick one. And I don't like knowing I still have a conscience, but I like the nightmares you've given me even less."

She wasn't prepared for such frankness, either. If that's what this was—with Zachary Denton, how did you tell? But with her pulse racing too fast, her body suddenly feeling too exposed in her leotards and tights, despite the shirt she'd tied around her waist, she found herself unable to trust what she was hearing.

"I…I'm sorry," she murmured. "It's been a tough day. I can't do this."

Despite hearing him call out her name, she crossed back to the kitchen counter and hung up the receiver. Breathing deeply, she then poured herself a glass of wine from Starla's bottle of chardonnay in the refrigerator.

Before she finished pouring, the phone rang again. She glanced out the kitchen window. Because of the valance curtains, she couldn't see him clearly, but enough to notice he was looking for her. Thanks to her dusty blue outfit and the full moon, it wasn't that difficult.

After returning the bottle to the refrigerator, she left the room, the phone continuing its ringing. It didn't stop until she shut off the living room light. Relieved, she flipped on the one at the foot of the stairs.

Just inside her bedroom, she hesitated. Once again she'd forgotten she'd left the night light on, and she'd opened the blinds for the African violets on the left night table. If she crossed to her bed or closet—anywhere—he would be able to see her. With the hall light behind her, no doubt he already could. She saw him easily enough.

The phone began ringing again.

"Damn it, Zach."

She slumped against the door and slid the cool glass across her overwarm forehead. This time she knew better than to hope it might be someone else. Taking another sip of wine didn't help her ignore it, either, nor did several seconds of meditational breathing exercises.

Fully intent on jerking the jack out of the wall, instead she picked up the receiver from the extension beside the violets. "Why are you doing this?" She hardly recognized her voice. Not even when she'd been jogging on the treadmill had she sounded this out of breath. Despite her suspicions of and concerns about Ger Sacks, she hadn't felt this pushed to an edge.

"Something's wrong. I want to help."

"Then stop calling."

"That's interesting coming from someone who's pushed herself into my business."

Yet another clip on the chin. Willa trapped the receiver between her chin and shoulder and rubbed at the throb that was starting at her temple. Maybe if she ignored him, he might get the message how she no longer felt inclined to do so.

"Talk to me, Willa. What's happened? Something has. You sound emotionally wiped out and look as if you've lost your best friend. Since word has it that you love your business and thrive under pressure, something fairly serious has to have happened. Combine that with the way you're dressed, my guess is that you ignored what I'd said and tried a bit of detective work on your own. Am I warm?"

"A friend wanted to try a temporary membership at the club. I agreed to go along for moral support." *And go ahead and ask me when I'll be ready to attempt anything like that again.*

"Even knowing that one of the men who worked there could be dangerous? Hell, woman, what's it going to take to make you listen?"

If it hadn't been for his husky voice, the way he leaned forward, looking so intent and...damn it, yes, concerned, she might have been able to keep her emotional distance. "I thought I could help both of us."

He sighed. "What happened?"

"I don't care to discuss it."

"Willa."

"It's *personal,* all right? It has nothing to do with you or your...situation."

"Fine. Tell me about it anyway because someone or something hurt you tonight, and you know full well that if you don't get it off your chest, you won't get any sleep."

The near gentleness in his tone threatened to shatter her armor. As it was, she had to set down her glass for fear of spilling the rest of her wine. "What are you, a warlock in your free time?"

"If I were, do you think I'd waste my time asking so many questions. What can I do to make you feel better?"

"Try humming a few bars of 'Tomorrow.'"

"Sorry. I never perform out of costume, and unfortunately my red wig is at the cleaners."

Willa smiled despite herself. "Yeah, no dog, either."

"No. He didn't survive the crash."

Willa clapped her hand over her mouth to hold back a gasp. How could she have forgotten that along with the rest, he'd lost a beloved pet? "Oh, Zach," she whispered, more miserable than ever. "I'm so sorry."

"Remind me to show you his picture sometime. Bear was one of a kind. Big, rude and totally unflappable."

"Be careful," she replied softly. "I may take you up on that invitation."

"Maybe I'm hoping you do."

CHAPTER TWELVE

Zach listened to the silence that followed and understood Willa's surprise and doubt. He had his own questions about what he'd just said. If anyone had magical powers, it was *her* because without his wanting her to, she'd managed to get through his defenses and made him respond.

"May I ask you a question?"

He reached for his glass, then stopped. No, he thought, he wouldn't hide this time.

"You can try. I don't promise I'll answer."

"It's not about you—well, not directly. It's about me."

"That sounds provocative."

"It does?"

Zach frowned. "Where's this sudden lack of confidence coming from?"

Her sigh sounded frustrated. "I don't like it either. All right, here goes…do you see me as a flirt?"

The sound that rose from deep in his chest was part growl and part laugh. "Anyone who goes around dressed like *that* has no right to ask such a question."

"This is important, Zach. Just because you know I have a business that focuses on making a woman feel beautiful and romantic, does that make you see me differently? Do I act as if I'm out to prove I can get any man I want?"

"Who suggested you were?" Zach replied, beginning to get a handle on this strange conversation.

"My assistant manager, who I'd also considered a dear friend. She's the one who asked me to go to the club with her. She thinks that working out there would help her meet more men." Willa tugged off her hair band, and then the protective band creating her ponytail.

"And after agreeing to go with her, you were the one who attracted the most attention, is that it?"

"Exactly." Willa paced from one corner of the window to the other. "I swear I didn't want that. I followed her from machine to machine, I listened, but let her ask all the questions. I even complimented her several times on her stamina. I know I was getting beat."

"Yet somehow you still made the fatal mistake of outshining her."

"But that's not true! I was simply *there*."

"Maybe she thought you could at least have fallen off one of the machines, been criticized for having dimpled thighs—something. How ungracious of you, Mrs. Whitney."

Willa uttered an exasperated sound. "I should have known better than to believe you were serious about helping."

"But I am," he assured her, aware she meant to hang up on him. "You're simply not listening. What I'm telling you is that this is her distortion of reality, not yours."

"Well, that so-called distortion sent her home in a huff, and now I have to wonder if she's going to speak to me again, let alone come back to work tomorrow."

"Mmm, but as Will Shakespeare warned in *Othello*, 'O! beware, my lord, of jealousy. It is the green-ey'd monster which doth mock the meat it feeds on.'" And, Zach mused, the more things changed, the more they stayed the same. "Sounds to me as if you'd be better off without her."

"But we've been a team since I started the store!"

"And through all that time you didn't notice her low self-esteem? That she set you up almost on a pedestal, often making *you* feel uncomfortable, only to occasionally use you as a brunt of a joke either to your face or behind your back?"

He had his answer in her silence. "Let me ask you one more thing. Was there someone there who particularly interested her? Someone she thought attainable for herself, but he paid *you* more attention than he did her?" Through the slits in the blinds, he watched Willa bite at her lower lip. "Come on, out with it."

"Gerald Sacks."

Ah, hell, he thought, he'd dug his pit and had fallen in. As the green monster took hold of him, he had to fight the violent urge to sweep his glass off his desk and across the room. Of any of the responses she could have made, he hadn't wanted to hear that one.

"Are…you…crazy? After what I told you, you two were toying around with *him?*"

The sound of the phone slamming sent a piercing pain through his head. He swore—but more at himself than for what she had done. He'd been a fool to explode. Even if she hadn't already been stinging from a painful experience, the quickest way to shut down communications was to mock the confidant. He may have failed in marriage, but he knew the rules.

Leave it be. He should never have phoned her anyway. His net was working, his situation was getting more dangerous. The note that had come in today's mail proved he may not have much time.

But for the moment he was safe, and she was so

close…so tempting. Just hearing her voice kept him from slipping too deep into the darkness and depression that threatened to keep him a prisoner forever.

Zach reached for the phone and punched in the number that was now committed to memory. It rang and rang…eight times, nine, ten. On the twelfth she picked up the receiver and set it down again. He couldn't see her actually doing it because she was out of view, somewhere to the left. He guessed she was sitting on her bed; that's where he'd watched the movers carry the mattresses and headboard.

He punched in the numbers again, and waited. Six… seven…eight…

"You're despicable."

He watched the window, willing her to move back to it. "Don't hang up. You know I'm going to apologize."

"Save it for someone who wants to hear it."

"You do. Otherwise you wouldn't have answered the phone."

"I answered so I could tell you what I thought of you," she shot back a bit too quickly.

"If that's what you want, why don't you come over and do it in person?" he drawled, fighting a unique anxiety stirring inside him.

Seconds later she appeared by the window and jerked up the blinds. "What did you say?"

"You heard me," he murmured, drinking in the sight of her. Blinds or no blinds, she made him wish a number of things, and want a great deal more. "What's the matter, cat got your tongue?"

"Isn't it amazing…all I have to do is mention a name like Ger Sacks and suddenly I get an invitation to the inner sanctum?"

"There's no connection tonight."

She shook her head. "Why, Zach?"

"The moon is full. I'm tired of fighting the obvious."

"I don't think so. Not you."

He had to polish off what was left in his glass to bring himself to say the words. "We've been working toward this since the moment we met, Willa."

"…your timing."

"What?"

"I said this isn't a good night to mention that."

"It's the best night. Someone tried to kick you in the teeth. Not because you deserved it, but because they were feeling sorry for themselves and it was easier to blame you than to work on their own problems. The worst thing you can do is to let them." He was speaking for both of them, but she didn't need to know that.

"You think the answer is to come over there instead?"

The tension coiling inside him threatened to snap something in his spine. "I suppose it is a ridiculous idea at that."

Willa uttered a soft gasp. "That's not what I meant, Zach."

"No?" He grimaced inwardly, hating the need he heard in that one small word.

"Is this strictly about you and me? Not…" She sighed. "What changed your mind?"

Ah. She'd been kind and hit him a fly ball. "Have you looked in a mirror lately?"

She inclined her head in a way that could have been a bow, agreement or a salute for cleverly answering the question with a question. "What's supposed to have changed my mind?"

"You mean is it safe to trust me?"

"Something like that. You've warned me off your-self. I might add, for more reasons than one."

"What's more, it's been quiet in town these past few days. Unnaturally so," he added, intentionally lowering his voice until he sounded like a radio actor in some matinee melodrama. "Do you suspect the beast is grow-ing restless? Maybe to play it safe he's going to pick on his neighbor as his victim?"

"Zach…" Willa ducked her head. "I don't think I'm up to this."

He dropped the theatrics and asked flat-out, "Is it the chair?"

"That's a terrible thing to suggest!"

He knew better than to take too much pleasure in her quick reply, but he did anyway. "Is it? I thought it rather honest myself. A woman has a right to expect that a man will give as much satisfaction as he takes. Considering my situation, it's only natural for you to have doubts about whether certain…things would be possible."

Willa moistened her lips. "No, you already made it clear that there wouldn't be any problem."

"Then why are you turning me down?"

"I'm feeling too…breakable tonight. If I came over there, it would be all of me, do you understand? Be-cause I don't know how else to be. And if you said or did anything…"

He was almost ready to beg, to vow that he would take her any way he could get her, and barely managed to stop himself. "You're right. Bad idea," he forced himself to say with a flippancy he'd never even known as a kid. "Well, it's time I get back to my mind games and gore anyway. Sweet dreams, fair Willa. Your watchdog on wheels is guarding the neighborhood as usual.''

"Zach?"

"Yeah?"

"Ask me again?"

"Who knows what tomorrow will bring?"

CHAPTER THIRTEEN

Zack waited until Willa lowered the blinds and shut them before he turned back to his computer. But the woman remained a vivid and powerful influence in his mind. It was the way he needed her to be tonight. He had work to do.

He'd already begun to breathe fictional life into her through his words. She had become independent, enticing Brett, brave but vulnerable Brett, who was fast becoming his protagonist's obsession. In the scene he'd been polishing before Willa had come home, he'd had Kane intent on seducing Brett, even though they'd barely known each other for more than a week. But as intrigued and effected as she'd been, she'd found his motives suspect, and he hadn't been able to convince her otherwise—understandable since what was going on inside him was complicated and contradictory. Women didn't react well to being pulled and pushed at the same time.

Zach smiled bitterly. "It's the same way on this side of the screen, Kane, old man."

Yes, understandable. But damned inconvenient.

Twisted by a malignant need for revenge, it had been Kane's cold-blooded intention to use Brett as an unwitting decoy to draw out flashy, conniving Jade. Once, Jade had been his partner, first his researcher, then his lover, then his wife—until Kane learned of the unscrupulous ways the insatiable, heartless Jade did research. When she'd learned his intent to divorce her, she'd tried to kill him and collect the insurance money, to inherit everything because he hadn't yet had time to change his will. But he'd fooled her. He'd survived.

Kane had let Brett believe he wanted her to stay away from Jade, then used their sexual chemistry to compel her to do otherwise. It was a despicable scenario for a character who had always written his novels with high ideals, no matter how seasoned they'd been with the macabre. Despicable, but again understandable. Because the tragedy that had taken away Kane's ability to walk, combined with the revelation about the subterfuge and betrayal by those he'd once cared for and trusted, had devoured his soul like a cancer-ravaging flesh.

"I feel sorry for you, you poor SOB," Zach muttered, pouring himself another drink. "Even if the romantics will accuse you of having lost sight of your moral values."

What Kane hadn't counted on was Brett herself. In a matter of days she'd effortlessly become his only link with his conscience, his lifeline to whatever shards that were left of his soul. And against his will she was regenerating it. Him.

He needed to sever the link between them if he wanted to continue, if he wanted to fulfill his goal for revenge. It meant tumbling even faster into the salivating jaws of madness, but he wanted that, too. There was nothing left for him in this world. Jade and her puppet had stained everything for him through their twisted perversions and greed.

"Write it," Zach ordered himself, settling his fingers over the keyboard. "After all, it's only fiction. This is where fact and fantasy separates, remember?"

Kane waited for the elevator to bring her up to him. He watched her through the filigree cage as she released the latch and slid aside the door. The bloodred rose was in her hand. It was stark against her white—

Zach swore. He'd intended to put her in red, but his subconscious, allied by the memory of his provocative conversation with Willa only days ago, had made him type in her preference instead. Fantasy, he reminded himself again. His fantasy. Grimly, he backspaced five times and typed in his choice.

—wine-red lace dress. Cut off the shoulders and narrow, it gloved her sleek form, and made his body stir with almost forgotten cravings.

"You couldn't stay away, could you?" The question was unnecessary, but he wanted her to say what he already knew, for the sake of hearing her voice one more time.

"If you'd wanted me to, then you shouldn't have sent this."

She stroked his cheek with the velvet petals. Oddly, they felt cold, like the finger of a corpse. Shivering, he tried to brush it away. A thorn caught his thumb.

When she noticed the droplet of blood, Brett slipped to her knees before him. "Let me," she whispered, and pressed her mouth to the wound.

Like warm, wet silk, her tongue glided over and around his flesh, triggering something primal and shockingly frantic in him. Driven by it, he closed his fingers around a fistful of her gold-and-silver hair and drew her upward until he could lock his mouth to hers.

She gasped in surprise and pain, and he thrust his tongue deep, stealing the sweetness he found there, driven…driven by the wild, too-long-denied emotions churning within him.

With his free hand he sought and kneaded her breast, lifted it. Then, yielding to another wave of feral passion, he ducked his head and opened his mouth over the generous curve swelling above the edge of lace.

She moaned and pressed herself to his searching mouth. Her willingness, eagerness only incited him.

"Closer," he demanded, easily lifting her over his lap.

She moved like grace itself and straddled the despised chair…but most shocking, she didn't seem repelled or disgusted. Humbled, grateful, he yielded to the joy that spawned a pleasure no passion ever had.

His touch reverential, he again traced the curves and hollows of her delectable body, this time drawing down lace, then suckling on first one, then the other taut breast he'd bared to his sight and his mouth. But no matter how much he tried to sate his unleashed hunger, it only made him want more of her. He wanted everything, release, the ecstasy only she could bring. To live a lifetime through a few moments in Brett's arms. Afterward, he would be able to bear anything.

Intent on slipping the dress completely off her, claiming all she was offering, he raised his head. Only then did he see the blood, terrible and everywhere. Where had it come from? Not from his wound. It wasn't possible.

Her mocking laughter filled him with dread. Looking up, he saw what he told himself wasn't possible. Judith, covered in blood and barely draped in what was left of Willa's dress.

"Did you think I'd let you have even one night with her, darling?" she taunted, wiping her bloodied hands on his shirt.

He tried to push her off him, but suddenly she was as strong as two men, her fingers digging sharply, painfully, into his flesh.

"Where is she?" he screamed. "What have you done with her? Willa!"

"Gone, sweetie. I gave her to him when I was through—"

Unnerved, Zach slammed the keyboard drawer into the desk and frantically pushed away from the computer. But he kept staring at the screen.

It was blank. He'd been typing, damn it, but somewhere along the way he must have...

How could it be blank?

How could everything become so twisted and confused, and *sick*.

Feeling like he'd been suckered by some hypnotist's crystal, he hyperventilated, trying to get air into his lungs, and get out whatever had affected him. Every breath was an agony. Sweat poured off him as though he were a sieve, and the salt stung his eyes. But he didn't care a bit about any of that. All he wanted to know was how this was possible.

The scene hadn't gone as planned. As if suddenly possessed, something else had controlled the direction of his thoughts. He hadn't even been aware of what was happening until he wrote—or thought he'd written—Judith's name. Willa's.

He raked his hands through his hair. He'd experienced bad moments before, and why not? As far as he was concerned, if a writer couldn't spook himself, what good was he? But he'd never terrified himself. Never nauseated himself.

He needed air...and space. It was safe, it had to be. Another minute locked in this place and he would lose his mind completely.

Desperate, he wheeled himself from the room and down the hall. Frantic, he jerked the elevator-cage door open and rolled himself inside.

Once downstairs he paused at a foyer closet beneath the stairs to grope in the near-total darkness for a pair of canes. Then he headed for the back door, and beyond it, the garage.

Willa hadn't been completely asleep. Between brooding over Starla's behavior and stunned by Zach's invitation, the sleep had eluded her. Not even a shower had helped. But she'd finally felt the welcome pull of slumber—only to be jarred awake by a metallic thump outside.

What was it? Was someone breaking into her van? Trying to steal it? No, it seemed to be coming more from the back. Could someone be trying to get into the house? During the past few days, she'd grown rather comfortable with the idea of having Zach awake all hours of the night. She figured the privacy-loving man was better than any watchdog.

Hoping he'd heard the noise, too, she jumped out of bed and went to the window. She knew better than to draw attention to herself by lifting the blinds. Shifting to the left side of the nearest window, she eased the blind back and snuck a peek. What she saw had her reeling.

Zach! He was walking!

The steps weren't ballet graceful let alone sidewalk normal; in fact he moved like the sweet old men who collected in the mall's center court to reminisce about better times and watch pretty girls. But thanks to the moonlight, she recognized the powerful build, and the Denton uniform of sleeveless sweatshirt and jeans. It was him, and he was doing what everyone, what *she,* thought was impossible.

Why had he kept this a secret? she wondered, as he shuffled toward the garage. And where was he going?

As if he felt her concentrated gaze, he paused and glanced over his shoulder. Willa knew the wisteria hid her fairly well, but she drew back for a moment just in case. When she looked again, he had the garage doors open.

Flabbergasted, she watched him back the dark blue or black van from the wood building and ease it down the driveway. The purr of the well-tuned engine also explained why he dared be this bold. She could barely hear it; if he'd been a few minutes later, she might never have been roused. It made her wonder how many times he'd done this since she'd moved in.

Willa sunk down to the floor and wrapped her arms around her knees, shaken to her core. She needed a minute to take this in. What's more, she truly meant to be happy for him—imagine, to be able to walk after what he'd been through!—but how did she keep from remembering his deceit? He'd lied to her. He'd let her—everyone for that matter—think he was trapped in his wheelchair. Why?

Willa frowned as she thought of something else. Did Ger Sacks know? He was Zach's trainer, for heaven's sake; how could Zach have kept it a secret? What about Judith? His ex-wife had said something about the van, but what? And what could this mean to Detective Pruitt and the investigation?

Had she been completely duped by the man? Was Judith right about him being an integral part of what had happened to Nancy Porter?

"No!" She rubbed at the goose bumps forming on her bare arms.

The mere possibility filled her with dread and hurt. It would mean she'd been more wrong about him than she'd ever been about anyone in her life. She couldn't accept it. He'd held her life in his hands...kissed her. He'd asked to make love with her.

Did she now have to wonder if the invitation had been something else? What if she'd said yes? Would she be alive right now?

"I can't let myself think that way."

And yet something had made him leave the sanctuary of his own four walls.

Willa buried her face in her hands. No way could she go back to bed now. Too many questions were racing through her mind, tying her stomach in knots; and more knots formed when she thought about how long he might be gone. She would go crazy waiting. She had to know what was going on.

Her insides rebelled as she pushed herself to her feet. Her fingers trembled as she snatched up her short cobalt-blue kimono and slipped it over the white teddy she'd worn to bed. But even when she pushed into her sneakers, she didn't let her nervousness affect her decision. Maybe this was reminiscent of the foolish, crazy, and most of all, dumb moves that had always turned her off of spooky movies. But she didn't see that she had a great number of options.

Fumbling for the flashlight she kept in her night-table drawer, she hurried downstairs. After checking the front and side windows to make sure he had definitely gone, she let herself out the back.

The light he'd left on up in his office helped guide her way, as did the moon, and Willa sprinted across his driveway to the back of his house. Her heart thumped when she saw the camera, but she reminded herself that in all probability he hadn't turned it on. Hoping she had the same luck with any alarms he might have set, she tested the doorknob, not surprised to find it locked.

"Okay, wise guy, now what?"

She would have to be an acrobat to reach the window beside the door, and although she thought it a reasonable guess, she didn't find a key hidden under the doormat, on top of the frame or secured beneath a rung of the wrought-iron railings.

She sighed because she'd reached the limit of her nerve. It would be one thing to take advantage of a discovered key, but she had to draw the line on breaking and entering. As it was, if her mother ever found out she'd been skulking around a neighbor's house at night when a crazy person was on the loose, the sweet sheltered soul would have a stroke.

Wondering what Zach's reaction would be if she stayed here and waited for him, Willa walked back down the ramp and looked up at the house. There was something to the direct approach; only, she couldn't quite picture him inviting her in. And if he had been hiding more than his ability to walk...

The only other thing she could think to do was check all the first-floor windows. Everything looked tightly secured, but this was an old house. Maybe one of the locks was loose.

She started on the driveway side because it kept her closer to her place which, silly or not, made her feel more secure. By the time she was on the front porch, though, she'd regained some confidence and moved quickly. Only when she reached the far end of the house did she decide she'd had enough. As much as she loved the woods by day, at night just the thought of who or what might be lurking in there, or in the tall grass, gave her the creeps.

Then why did you bother coming out at all?

Another good point. She had to finish what she'd started, or be prepared to live with the doubts.

Less than a minute later, she realized how close she'd come to missing an incredible opportunity when she discovered the first window's lock was completely disengaged.

This had to be a trap. Every old cliché raced through her mind as she shoved up the heavy glass and drew aside the brocade draperies to peer inside, and she agreed with them all: there were no free lunches...she was concerned about getting what she'd asked for...she believed that if you wanted to play, you had to pay. This was simply too bizarre. Zachary Denton forgetting to lock a window?

Willa tried to forget all that as she hoisted herself up and over the ledge. It proved harder than expected, thanks to her earlier workout that now had every muscle in her body protesting. Easing one leg between the drapes, she tested the area for any furniture. Finding nothing, she set her foot on the hardwood floor and crab walked her way inside.

The beam of her flashlight picked up dark paneling like that in the foyer, and equally dramatic paintings. Willa wished there was time to linger and study Zach's collection, but settled for a brief, longing look at a huge one of a lighthouse under the siege of a stormy sea before checking out the rest of the room. This had to be the study. Between most of the paintings were floor-to-ceiling bookshelves, and all were jammed with everything from hardcovers to paperbacks to magazines. She could tell Zach had no need of Vilary's public library; he'd amassed an inventory that put the town's to shame.

She paused at the table in the center of the room, drawn by the marble chess set. She knew virtually nothing about the game, save the name of a few pieces and the general goal, but it looked to her as if Zach was in the middle of a contest. Pausing beside the table she considered the white queen who appeared dangerously threatened by the black queen along with—was that a bishop? Something about the challenging positions, the odds, made her reach up to her throat. Without understanding strategy, she knew the poor white queen was in trouble. Why wasn't her king moving from behind his army to protect her?

Deep in concentration, the abrupt ringing of a phone

somewhere behind her and out in the foyer—not to mention the hint of a few others upstairs—sent her lurching into the table. A few pieces tipped over. Several more wobbled precariously.

"Oh, damn…damn!" Horrified, she tried to steady what she could, but when they stopped teetering, she bit her lower lip at the damage. What on earth was she supposed to do? All three of the center pieces were on their sides. Had the black queen been two or three spaces ahead of the first line of combatants? Had her bishop been one space behind her or one over to her right? She had to choose carefully; Zach would be able to tell if she guessed incorrectly.

"You'd think he would own an answering machine," she muttered under her breath as she reset the pieces.

Just when she thought the house would never be silent again, the ringing stopped, and although she was ready to call the whole thing off, she forced herself to head out to the foyer. She suspected that any answers about Zach would be found upstairs in his office and it would be wise to get moving.

The stairs creaked more than she remembered from last time, and she didn't dare hold on to the banister on the way up. Her palms were sweating so badly, the police wouldn't need to bother bringing in a fingerprinter to ID her. Not that Zach was apt to invite the police in here.

His office was another dark, book-packed room, but far messier than downstairs, which made Willa wonder for the first time who cleaned up for him? Of course, from the condition of the place she figured no one did. The wastebasket looked as if it had begun overflowing around Wednesday, and a near-empty bottle of Scotch would soon join the mess, sending a new wave of paper and wrappers scattering across the floor. The walls were punctured and scarred from all the pictures and maps that had been taped and tacked up over the years. She supposed he used the visuals as a reference and for inspiration. Right now he seemed to be focusing on photos of chessboards. Then there was a mysterious photo involving leather and chains she didn't want to look at too closely, and one of the universe featuring what she thought was a black hole. But what really caught her attention, was the magazine ad of the blond nude photographed through a window.

Willa turned to look out his window toward her place. There was no ignoring the parallels that came to mind. But had he chosen to hang a picture because it reminded him of her or, like the stalker, did he possess a predilection for blondes? Inevitably, she remembered Judith and decided this wasn't the best time emotionally to dwell on that.

Turning her back on the scene, she circled the desk to peek at the computer screen. She was disappointed to find it blank, and she didn't know enough about computers to try to retrieve his directory let alone look into any file. Just as well, she told herself; she wasn't here to peek at his latest bestseller anyway. What she wanted were the notes from the stalker.

She flipped through the loose-leaf notebook on Zach's desk, tempted to smile when she noticed his atrocious penmanship. But his doodles sobered her. He drew too many depressing symbols, hangman's nooses, daggers and tombstones with RIP written on them.

Shaking her head, she shifted her focus to the desk drawers, difficult to open because they, too, were filled to overflowing. She sifted through inch after inch of receipts, catalogs, rubber bands, paper-clip chains, wrinkled and ripped magazine clippings of his reviews, crushed granola and chocolate bars, and assorted notebooks filled with more doodles and notes.

Lulled to near complacency, finding the handgun in the top drawer was a blow. It was silly, really, since not only A.J. had owned one, but so did her father. And to be fair, she could understand Zach wanting the protection. She just wished she hadn't found it.

The important thing is that he hadn't taken it with him.

Heartened by that thought, she continued her hunt. She learned a good deal about Zach from snooping. He didn't smoke, but he had a weakness for junk food. He clearly drank too much, though she'd never noticed it in his voice or behavior. The unfilled prescriptions she found moments later in the back of the drawer suggested part of the reason was to avoid taking the pain pills, and wise or not, her heart went out to him again.

Besides being a slob, he was also a pack rat, even keeping a beer coaster with a phone number, which she doubted, if asked, he could explain. But it was his dark side that both intrigued and troubled her. He seemed obsessed with anything that had to do with fear, death and the paranormal. Even the piece of driftwood on his desk that served as a paperweight had an eerie quality to it. It looked like an arm rising out of the surf, almost beckoning. How could anyone spend so much time around all this and not be drawn in? Drawn down?

They can't. When is that going to sink in?

Blinking to fight the sudden burning in her eyes, she straightened the blotter she'd accidently nudged out of position. As she pushed it back onto the desk, she noticed some papers beneath. Her pulse immediately started racing.

Yes, this was it. There were almost a dozen, worn from a great deal of handling. The first three read like letters; expansive and adoring, they were written by someone who knew Zach's work intimately. Fan mail, Willa thought, wincing at the almost painful and gushing praise. For *The Well* he wrote, "You know me. You know what I've suffered and what they did to me. Thank you for saying it was all right to make them pay. Always, your devoted reader."

Willa shuddered, wondering what payment the reader had exacted for his real or imagined pain. It was incredible to think how long he'd worked on the letter, painstakingly cutting to keep his anonymity.

It was the third note that showed the most disturbing slant, a change toward intent. Short and heartbreaking, it said only, "She's found me. So beautiful and terrible. I'm afraid. Help me."

By the fourth communication, the transformation was done. Truth had been twisted and bitterness thrived. "You never cared about me. I hate you. You'll pay. Wait and suffer!"

But the last, the most wrinkled, as if it had been crushed in a palm and then smoothed out again, produced the most heart-thumping reaction. "We've found the one. Her time is close. Do you want to beg me to spare her?"

Willa had to shove the papers back under the blotter. Just touching them made her stomach roll. But it was the flash of headlights that locked the breath in her throat.

Zack was back!

CHAPTER FOURTEEN

She'd never moved so fast in her life. Almost knocking Zach's computer monitor off his desk, Willa lunged to get away from the window and raced out of the room. Running blindly down the hall, she groped for and found the banister and stumbled halfway down before her terror-stricken mind let her realize what was wrong.

She'd forgotten her flashlight.

Where did I put it?

Frantic, she scrambled back up the stairs and, before she could stop, she kicked the thing across the room. The terrible crash had her cringing—surely, Zach had heard *that*—but it was the pain in her foot that made her clench her teeth and whimper. Nevertheless, she dropped to all fours and reached under the desk to where it had rolled.

Once she had it again, she retraced her steps, knowing that she couldn't risk using the light. She didn't want to think what Zach would do to her if he found her in here. On the other hand, it might not matter; the way her heart was pounding, she was going to die of terror any second now.

The back door opened as she reached the bottom of the stairs. She froze, although everything inside her screamed for her to run. But if she ran, he would hear—and what if he had two guns and had taken one with him?

Easy. Easy. Take it one tiptoe at a time.

She waited for the first board to creak. Sweat should

have broken out on her brow from the tension vibrating within her. One step, two, three... She inched toward the study, while every atom of her being listened to him shutting and bolting the back door, groaning as he settled into his chair. The thump and soft clanging sound that followed she identified as his setting down the canes.

But once she made it into the room and felt the closeness of freedom, the impulse to hurry affected her direction and balance. Combined with the lack of light, she tragically miscalculated where the chess table had been.

She felt part participant and part observer, and knew she had no chance. The instant her thigh came in sharp contact with hard wood, she gasped, then everything— table, chair, board and a few dozen hunks of marble— went flying, and she followed.

Between the pain and her cry, she didn't hear another thing until lights blinded her and he swore a blue streak.

"Do you have a death wish? Is that your problem?" he roared in conclusion.

"Why don't you just use that thing and get it over with," Willa sobbed back, breathless and hurting. She supposed he'd expected the worst and had grabbed the first thing he could get his hands on as a weapon. Right now an added blow from a wooden meat mallet didn't seem all that painful.

"I should." But he tossed it into a corner by the door and wheeled toward her. "And then I should wring your neck. You don't want to come over when you're invited—no. But it's okay to break into my house?"

"I didn't break in."

"The damn doors were locked!"

"Well, that window wasn't!"

He followed her trembling, but pointing finger to the window on the left, and his scowl deepened. "The hell you say. I never leave those open." But he wheeled over to inspect it, whipping aside the heavy drapes and running his hands alongside the paneling. Finally he slammed it shut and secured the lock.

When he pushed himself back to her, he had a strange look on his face. "Don't lie to me, Willa."

"Ho-ho, you're one to talk."

To her surprise, his expression turned guilty, even apologetic. But there was a little resentment, too.

"You saw."

"There was a crash. I woke up."

"I fell." He bowed his head. "Damned clumsy ox, that's all I am now."

Dear heaven, is that how he thought of himself? "Zach, maybe it's not the way you wanted things to turn out, but you can *walk*. Why can't you see how fantastic—what a blessing that is?"

"You call half dragging yourself for a few dozen yards walking? And the pain so bad, you'd as soon take a gun to your head a blessing?"

"Yes, you embittered jerk! If I could have had my husband back in that shape, I would have thanked God every day for the rest of my life!"

He looked stunned, but no more amazed than she was at herself. She'd never admitted anything like that before, and no doubt A.J. would have acted no better than Zach; however, now that the words were out she knew they were her truth. She and A.J. would have been okay. She would have bullied him with love until it *was* okay. Life was simply too precious to wish away or ignore, as Zach seemed determined to prove.

Sniffing back the unwanted tears of emotional and

physical pain, she tried to stand, but the pain in her thigh and hip hadn't lessened one bit. She did well just to sit up. Biting back a moan, she tugged her kimono down over her thighs and retied the loose sash, disgusted that on top of everything else she was making a spectacle of herself.

"That's a nasty bruise on your thigh."

"It's okay."

Zach shifted closer, then locked his wheels and extended his hand. "Come on."

He'd caught her sneaking around in his house; did he think she was going to trust him? Especially when he was looking at her like he couldn't decide whether she should be lunch or fishing bait? She shook her head. "I'll be fine."

He didn't answer; rather, he reached over and swept her off the carpet and onto his lap as if she were a dropped towel. It reminded her again—as if she needed reminding—of what kind of strength she was dealing with.

"Zach, this is crazy. Let me— What are you doing?"

Without so much as an "Excuse me" or "May I?" he parted and pushed up her kimono. Her throbbing flesh suddenly felt scorched when he ran his fingers over the bruise.

"That needs ice."

"I'll put some on as soon as I get home."

But when she tried to get off him, the arm tightened around her waist. He used his other hand to release the brake. Willa knew she should be grateful that his overall reaction hadn't been worse, but being this close to him was more than her confused and vulnerable emotions needed right now.

"Zach, please. Let me go."

"I told you, the window is always locked. At least it's supposed to be," he replied, as if explaining simple addition to a child. "What do you think that means?"

"Your cleaning lady was trying to air out the place and forgot to close it?"

"I don't have a cleaning lady."

"Really? You could have fooled me."

He made a faint sound deep in his chest, but she didn't know whether it was a snort or a chuckle. When he didn't go to the kitchen, but turned toward the elevator, she also didn't care.

"What are you doing?"

"You need ice."

"But the kitchen's that way," she said, hooking her thumb over her left shoulder.

He nodded, but kept going, never once looking at her. "And I'm telling you that someone who'd been in my house deliberately left that window unlocked. Now I'm going to ask you one more question," he said, sliding open the cage door. "Did you find what you were looking for?"

"Yes."

"Did you read all of them?"

"Yes," she admitted more softly. Oh, Lord, she didn't want to put it all together.

"Then how do you think I could let you go back out there in the darkness, alone, knowing that some demented...monster might be waiting for you?"

Was she the one, then? Willa decided she didn't want an answer to that. She couldn't handle it at the moment. But as he slid the door shut and the elevator growled and rose, she knew the answer stood fatalistically between them.

She looked down at her hands that were fidgeting

with the end of her sash, rolling and unrolling. It amazed her. She never fidgeted. "Where did you go, Zach?"

"For a ride."

"Do you do that often?"

"Only when I reach out to a woman I've been trying to resist, and she tells me to get lost."

"I didn't!"

"Well, either way, you weren't coming over." He sighed. "I thought I could be philosophical about it. I even told myself it was what I'd wanted. Instead, the walls started closing in on me. The writing... Things weren't going well. I figured that being out in the night, rolling down the windows and chasing the stars would help."

"Did it?"

"Didn't get that far. I started feeling uneasy about leaving, so I turned around and came back."

And scared her half to death. "I'm sorry for knocking over your chess set."

"No, the game needed to be stopped. I didn't like the pattern that was forming."

"Me, neither. I felt sorry for your white queen. She looked as if she were about to get slaughtered."

"Yes." The elevator stopped and for the first time since lifting her off the floor, Zach looked into her eyes. "But do you understand? If I hadn't come back, I'm not sure you would have gotten out of here alive."

Her mind resisted the idea forming, the concept that someone read her so well that she'd been set up to come here tonight. If she'd been killed, Zach would naturally have been the police's prime suspect.

"No." Shock came like a series of shattering waves and, needing to anchor herself to something real and solid, Willa wrapped her arms around his neck. "Oh, Zach!"

His arms closed around her, fierce, but wonderfully reassuring. Burying her face in the warm curve of strong neck and shoulder, she held tight. She didn't even mind his silence, or that when the elevator came to a stop, that he had to let go to open the door and wheel them out. It was enough to draw from his confidence and power. When she was this close, she knew how wrong she'd been to have any doubts or fear about him. Zach might get furiously angry with her, but he would never hurt her.

Only when she felt a draft of cold air did she look around. "You have a refrigerator in your bedroom."

Incredible. A smile tugged at her lips because it wasn't one of those hotel-room-size ones, either. In fact, half the wall across from his giant bed was set up as a kitchen, and the other half had every piece of electronic equipment he could want.

"Except for your office, is every room in this place dark?" This room wasn't paneled; rather, it was papered with an intense sapphire blue, and the furnishings were all heavy bold mahogany.

"I guess. I haven't really thought about it except for in here," he said, taking a container of ice and placing several cubes in the towel on the counter. "I don't sleep during normal hours, and this side of the house gets sun most of the day."

Willa doubted that any sunlight made it through the heavy blue drapes on the two sets of windows. Her gaze wandered back to the bed, which was unmade, but the sheet and spread were rolled back neatly. She could see the impression of his body on the dramatic green-and-burgundy sheets, which immediately triggered intimate, erotic images in her mind. That made her react all the sharper when Zach laid the ice pack against her thigh.

"That's worse, not better!" she cried, trying to remove it.

"You just need to focus on something else," Zach said, cupping the back of her head with his free hand and claiming her mouth with his.

He was right. The feel of his lips against hers definitely emptied her mind of everything but him and the realization that she'd been wanting to be this close again.

She clenched at the sweatshirt so hot from his body, and thrilled to the feel of the deep breath he took in response to that. She thrilled, too, when he didn't linger on tentative nibbles and brushstrokes. As if he'd expected never to get this close again, he parted her lips and drove his tongue deep.

Maybe it was part adrenaline, a result of once again having been made too aware of life's fragility. More than likely it was because no one kissed like Zachary Denton. All honesty and bold passion, he made no excuses for his desire, didn't hide it behind coaxing kisses, or tentative darts and teasing strokes. He kissed as if she were melting ice cream and he didn't want to miss one drop.

When he paused, it was only to breathe and whisper, "Wrap your arms around me. Hold me." Then he locked his mouth to hers again and took on the erotic dance where he'd left off.

The soft thud of the ice cubes tumbling to the carpet came as no surprise. Willa thought it impressive that Zach had managed to keep focused and hold them in place for as long as he did. Nor did she miss the damp cool cloth as it slid off her. With Zach combing his hands into her hair and intensifying the kiss, any residual discomfort was reduced to an abstract awareness.

Then just as she thought they might melt into each other, he groaned, and rocked his forehead against hers. "Don't say no. I can't let you go this time."

Madness. Now she knew she'd left most of her senses next door, and had lost the rest when creeping through his window. It no longer mattered that they were veritable strangers, that he troubled her almost as much as he tempted her. This moment was about instincts and fate, and right now theirs were mysteriously, irrevocably tied.

"Tell me what to do."

"Anything and everything you want," he murmured, stroking his hands down her back. "I know I'm going to try." As if to prove it, he shifted to her front and untied her kimono's belt. But after slipping the silk from her shoulders, he swallowed. "Damn."

Her weakness had long been wanting sensual things close to her skin, even when her outer clothing consisted of functional cotton, even casual T-shirts and leggings. The disadvantage was that mesmerized stares such as Zach's had a decided physical effect on her that was impossible to hide, so that when he reached out and brushed his fingers across her already taut nipples, she reacted to the excruciating sweetness as if he'd plunged a dagger into her breasts.

Every muscle in Zach's face worked. "Would you consider a big favor?"

Thinking her jerky response had hurt him, she asked, "Do you need me to get up?"

"Only so I can look at you."

Even if she had been shy, she could never have denied him that request, not once she saw his expression.

When he lifted her to her feet and gazed at her, she thought it amazing how arousing a visual caress could be.

But looking wasn't enough when Zach focused on her bruise. Taking gentle but firm hold of her hips, he leaned forward and kissed the already discoloring bump. Before the tingling sensations had begun to dance from nerve ending to nerve ending, he'd inched up the teddy to do the same to the bruise forming on her hip. Then he slipped both hands into the silky material to cup her and draw her closer.

As he pressed his face against her womb, her knees turned weak. Stroking his hair, she murmured, "Zach...let's lie down."

Never taking his eyes off her, he backed his chair to the side of the bed and locked the wheels. Willa wondered if she should offer to help, but realized that in doing this every day, he'd become quite adept at it.

It also became apparent how few words were necessary between them. With a look, she knew he welcomed her helping him take off his things, and that after she slipped off her sneakers, his faintest touch told her that he wanted to finish undressing her himself.

But it wasn't as if they didn't speak. Zach whispered accolades to her hair when it brushed his thighs, oaths when she explored him with her hands and mouth, and a two-worded prayer when he eased the straps of her teddy off her shoulders and drew the garment to her waist, hips and beyond.

In his own way, he was also graceful, although she knew he didn't think so. But his weight training had made him extremely conscious of his body, and like some Eastern martial-arts master, he rarely moved without purpose. As a result, the lines and angles his body formed made him as beautiful to her as she seemed to be to him—something apparent as they shifted back against the pillows. Every gesture, every exploration was based on some sixth sense of what the other craved or needed.

And always there were the kisses—long, drugging, hot, hungry. Through them they gauged the mounting pulse of their passion, until glistening with sweat and feverish with longing for more, for everything, Zach coaxed her on top of him.

"You realize what a risk this is," he warned softly, although his eyes relayed the message that he would die if she changed her mind.

Willa could think of two or three things he could mean, but she'd already come to peace with all of them. Slowly, ever so slowly, she eased herself down, careful as she took him into her body. They had already stretched the waiting beyond bearable. "We'll talk about it...later," she whispered back.

After that she couldn't have spoken if she'd wanted to because where there had been hunger and passion, now there was desperation. Obsession. They didn't explore, they clung and rode...existed on one breath... reached for one summit.

In the last second they looked into each other's eyes. Hope, fear, yearning...all were there, along with something fragile and new. Murmuring unintelligibly, Zach sought a final kiss. Seconds later, Willa felt him explode inside her and, gasping, she surrendered to her own release.

It was beyond perfect, and she understood now that this had all been inevitable. They were too sexually attuned to have escaped each other. But in the peace and tremulous silence that followed, she wasn't prepared for the added gift of wonder that shimmered sweetly between them.

CHAPTER FIFTEEN

"Is it later yet?" Zach murmured, unable to take his eyes off the woman lying beside him. He hadn't really wanted to ask. Already his body, too long denied such pleasure, was responding to her closeness, while his mind, rarely at peace at the best of times, waged silent war with known and unknown monsters.

Willa rose on one elbow, her expression luminous and gentle. "I didn't mean to sound mysterious. I just didn't want to ruin the mood."

He couldn't decide what he found more stimulating: her slow, slightly wicked smile, or her soft, feminine voice. The fantasy of watching the former and listening to the latter for the rest of his life was extremely appealing and, therefore, dangerous. He had to temper the panic that caused by sucking in a deep breath.

"You shouldn't have put yourself at risk for me," he said, once again lured by the silky feel of her hair.

"But did I, Zach? Neither one of us has been with anyone in years. What's more, during your time in the hospital, they would have discovered if you were ill. You would have told me."

Of course he would. But that wasn't what he'd meant. "What about birth control?"

"I was on the Pill when A.J. died We wanted a bit more time to enjoy each other before we thought about starting a family. After...well, I was an emotional and physical wreck. My doctor thought it best if I kept taking them." Again the smile crept out. "Ironically, I'm on my last prescription. She's decided it's time I consider other options.''

She would be a wonderful mother—nurturing and yet strong enough to let her children experiment, take risks and grow. He, on the other hand, wouldn't know where to begin caring for a son or daughter. Hell, half the time he did a lousy job of trying to take care of himself.

''That wasn't a proposal, Zach.''

He'd once read of an old witch doctor who claimed that when a man poured himself into a woman, it made him transparent. He'd never had reason to believe that until tonight.

''You shouldn't be wasting your time on me. You deserve someone who could give you a full life. Children. A normal home.'' The more he admitted to her, the tighter his throat became. The more he needed to touch her. ''I'm not even sure I ever knew what 'normal' was.''

He expected his confession to upset her; after all, what rat seduced a woman, and only afterward warned her that he wasn't worth an emotional investment? Instead, she continued watching him in that calm, serene way that turned his insides into a knot.

''I'll put an ad in the paper advertising for that, first thing Monday morning.''

She was right; he did sound like a jerk who was pretending to be noble. But he knew himself too well. ''I come with a lot of baggage, Willa.''

''Most people do. What makes you think yours is so unmanageable?''

He didn't know if he could put it into words. He'd never told this to anyone. ''As a kid I had an ordinary family life, in an ordinary small town in Pennsylvania— or so it seemed. My father was the area's only vet, my mother helped him and I was the model son. No one ever held it against us for not going to church on Sundays because there were always patients to attend to and emergencies out at someone's farm. No one ever thought it odd when a beloved pet didn't survive an operation or that my father always volunteered to find homes for unwanted litters. People were simply glad to be rid of them.''

Willa's expression turned wary. "What did he do with them?"

He hesitated, knowing it would be the last time she would ever look at him quite the same way. "Sacrificed most. Ate some."

"No. Oh, no, Zach!"

She sat up and whirled away. Zach watched her take several deep breaths, press her hand to her mouth. She was so beautiful with her silver-and-gold hair shimmering down her back in sexy disarray, the long, elegant line of her back. But her shoulders were rigid with tension, her spine ready to snap. He waited, not knowing what she would do next, nor certain how to go on. He only knew that she couldn't be any more ashamed, or despise him more than he loathed himself.

When she finally faced him again there were tears of compassion in her eyes. Not horror, he thought in amazement.

"How did you bear it?"

"Who said I did?" Could he dare believe what he was seeing? Hearing? "Even my earliest memories, when I was four or five, I remember it sickened me, and I tried to resist when they made me participate in the rituals. But they punished me."

"How?"

"I'll never burden you with those details."

"Zach—"

"Never, Willa. The point is that if I wanted to survive, I had to submit. Sometimes I still have nightmares, wake up sick to my stomach and terrified." Just talking about it had him breaking out in a sweat, so cold, so different than what he'd experienced when they'd made love.

"Let me get you something." Willa slipped off the bed. "Is there a beer in the refrigerator?"

"There's Scotch on the counter. With or without ice, it doesn't matter."

It helped watching her, noting her unselfconsciousness, how her concern was all for him. What had he done to deserve this? Feeling an uncharacteristic lump in his throat, he sat up and bunched the pillows. "Thanks," he mumbled, avoiding her eyes when she returned with the bottle and a tumbler filled with ice.

"Don't think I want you to drink the whole thing."

He made a face as he poured. "So you've seen that I prefer taking my nourishment in liquid form?"

"You can't keep producing all you do while drinking like that, Zach."

"Yeah, well, living to a ripe old age so some TV weatherman can flash a picture of me with a birthday cake resembling a brushfire gone out of control, isn't an inducement to hang around, honey." He tried not to think of the downstairs window, and how grateful he was to be alive, to have followed his instincts and come back to the house.

He'd barely taken a generous swallow when Willa took the glass and bottle away and set them on the night table. "If you're going to talk like that, I'm going to ration you. Now go on. Tell me how you escaped."

"You don't ever escape. You can't. Not your memories."

"You survived," Willa said, taking his hand in both of hers. "What's more, you *want* to survive, despite the shame and the haunting memories. I see it, Zach. It's in your eyes when you look at me."

Dear God, if he was dreaming, he never wanted to wake up. "You're one sharp cookie, Mrs. Whitney."

"And stubborn. Tell me the rest," she coaxed, squeezing his hand.

It helped to focus on their linked fingers. "When I was nine, after one of my attempts to run away, they let it slip that I was adopted." As if it were yesterday, he recalled the strange mixture of relief and fury he'd felt at the time. "It filled me with rage—well, as much rage as a nine-year-old can muster for a system that was so careless about putting a child into a home they hadn't investigated thoroughly. After that, I became obsessed with escaping. Two months later I did."

"Did you report them to the police?"

He smirked. "Only the first time I ran away. I never made that mistake again."

With a moan, Willa shifted to brush his hair off his forehead and to kiss him there. "I can't bear to think of how it was for you being all alone with nowhere to go, trusting no one."

"It was heaven compared to where I'd been. Oh, it had its scary moments—I stole as much money as I could, but a few days later I got rolled and beaten up pretty badly. But after that I stayed away from cities, learned to travel at night to avoid the law who kept wanting to put me in juvenile homes." He chuckled to himself. "Ten minutes around me and you knew I wasn't a candidate for a foster home, let alone adoption."

"What about school? How did you manage?"

"I never went to formal school again. As for surviving, I became a proficient thief." He shrugged, not proud of it, but knowing at the time there had been no other way for him. "Then I found Lotty. This was in Tennessee and I was about…eleven. She was a retired schoolteacher. A sweet, sweet black woman, big as she was tall. She worked the acreage her husband had toiled over until he'd died of exhaustion." Zach smiled, finally feeling the easing of the tension and coldness that always came when memories hurled him into the past.

"She took you in."

He nodded. "And that tells you how brave she was because I was one tough customer. Wild. Sick, too…and I'm not just talking physically. She saved my life, pulled me back from the edge of madness—" *from the valley of the shadow of death* "—and she gave me an education."

"So that's where your gift for storytelling came from," Willa said, lowering herself to his chest and kissing him over his heart. "Oh, I know I would have loved her. How long were you two together?"

"Almost five years. One night she gave me a volume of Edgar Allan Poe's stories. Said she'd prayed for a long time to the good Lord to stop my nightmares and screaming. Seeing as He hadn't seen fit to do that, it struck her that maybe I was supposed to use them somehow. Then she went to bed and passed away in her sleep." He'd cried like a baby, and although she'd said numerous times that the farm had been willed to him, he'd left right after her funeral. It was years before he returned, after he'd been published and had started to climb on the charts. By then he knew the right thing to do with the property, and signed it over to a young newlywed couple, relations of Lotty's friends and closest neighbors.

"Now you know," he said, stroking Willa's hair.

"Did you ever find out about...?"

"There was a fire and he died." Zach still refused to call the man who'd adopted him by name. "No one seems to know what happened to her. I hope they're both burning in hell with their *master*.

Willa immediately sat up, and grasped his shoulders. "Don't, Zach. Don't let the bitterness and pain own a part of you anymore."

"It is a part of me," he nearly shouted, exasperated that she hadn't listened. "That's what I've been explaining to you. Bitterness, pain, fear, madness...they feed my work, and eat at me all at the same time. You want to understand me? Understand that I've faced death more than most lead-footed drivers deal with traffic tickets. I've been beaten and tortured, manipulated and threatened. I know what it is to look into the faces of the most despicable and soulless human beings and understand them. And I can't stop writing about any of it or them," he ground out, "because they're still out there—the Judiths and the stalkers and the satanists and child abusers...all the monsters who look so damned safe. So trusting. So normal!"

"That doesn't mean you're like them. You're *not* crazy!" she cried back.

He couldn't yell at her anymore. It turned his stomach to see what that did to her. But saving her from what was outside *and* himself remained his priority. "I will go over the edge, Willa," he replied, resigned. "Do you know when that day will be? When whoever's out there gets to you. And as long as you have anything to do with me, they'll try.''

"I'm not turning my back on you, Zach.'' She touched his cheek, his lips. "After this is over, you can put steel bars on your windows and dig a moat around your house to keep me out. But until then I'm not letting you wait in the dark alone.''

"Then heaven help us both,'' he moaned, dragging her closer and locking his mouth to hers.

This wasn't the way he planned things to go. He'd lost. He'd failed in making her realize what a mistake she was making. And yet losing had never filled him with such relief or felt this good. Later, somehow, he would have to make her see reason. But just once more he wanted to experience the sweet, hot ecstasy of loving her.

As before, merely kissing her intoxicated him. He couldn't get enough, whether he crushed her against him, framed her face with his hands to hold her still for his hungry plundering or plowed his fingers into her hair and tilted back her head to feast on every inch of her face and throat.

But Willa, too, seemed swept away by the wild current of their passion. He'd only started to reexplore her sleek curves, hadn't begun to sate himself on the full taut breasts that fanned his flaming imagination when she reached down to take him in her hand. "Come inside me. Now. I want to hold you.''

She stole his heart and his soul. Feeling control slipping away, he could only hold fast as she rocked and undulated against him. "Willa...sweet...please... *please*.''

They came apart in each other's arms, crying and

gasping. And in that moment he knew life had never been more precious to him.

She fell asleep quickly. He couldn't. Comfortable though he was, sated, as happy as he dared be, Zach's racing mind would give him no peace.

He was falling in love, and it was wonderful.

But it was terrible, too, for on the heels of that revelation came the oppressive feelings that had driven him out of his house earlier in the evening, and they were returning with a vengeance. Bringing with them new ones, as well.

He had to stop the madness, stop Judith, but how? Damn it, *who* was her puppet?

Somewhere outside he heard a shrill scream. He shivered and instinctively tightened his arms around Willa because whatever it was, it had sounded almost human—or rather inhuman.

An owl, he told himself. Or a coyote. It was merely the night that toyed with the imagination; in that respect, he agreed with what one of his favorite poets, Ranier Maria Rilke, once wrote. Darkness *did* pull in everything. It made it its own and, therefore, mysterious. That's all.

But after turning off the light and again attempting to sleep, the red-eyed demons behind his closed lids mocked and taunted his confidence and resolve. Resigned to a long night, he decided that at least he could watch Willa sleep in his arms.

Even that, however, didn't keep him from listening just in case there was a repeat of that unholy cry.

CHAPTER SIXTEEN

Willa fought yet another yawn as the phone rang. "Good afternoon, Whimsy," she said into the receiver, glad this was Sunday. They'd only opened minutes ago, and it was a relatively short day compared to weekdays—a good thing, since she'd only managed a minimum of sleep last night at Zach's.

"Mrs. Whitney? Willa? This is Judith Denton."

Nothing and no one could have chased away her grogginess faster. Willa gripped the curved edge of the check-out counter until the wood creaked in protest. "Yes, Mrs. Denton. What can I do for you?"

"What do you think?"

Willa had expected a bold response, even a blunt one, but hardly this. "Excuse me? I'm not sure I understand."

"I tried to call you at home earlier, but apparently you weren't there."

No, she hadn't. At least not for longer than it took her to shower and dress for work. Before that she'd spent the morning making Zach his first real breakfast in who knew how long.

"I'm sorry I missed your call. What's this about?"

"Haven't you read the papers this morning? Watched the news?"

The woman's attitude was truly trying. But because of her new closeness with Zach, Willa was determined to know what Judith was up to. "No. Between moving and catching up on things here, I'm afraid I've fallen behind on local goings-on. But you're obviously trying to tell me something, so maybe you should get to the point."

"There's been a murder."

She didn't know what to say. "Excuse me? Do you mean your friend...?"

"No. Bless her, Nancy's still in a coma, but holding on. This was another unfortunate soul. She was found near the creek around the corner from your street. You didn't see the police on your way to the mall? I would imagine someone will be out there most of the day collecting evidence."

Willa knew the spot she was referring to; only a quarter of a mile before her street, Cox Creek had a short bridge that transversed it. But the creek was more of a mosquito patch than a tributary, until it poured; then it became a body of water to be respected. "No. I took a shortcut. Are the police certain the two incidents are linked?"

"She has the same kind of markings on her neck that Nancy does, and her underwear is missing. You won't read that in the paper. Detective Pruitt told me when he came to break the news."

Although Willa had been anticipating Starla's arrival, the moment she swept into the store with her nose in the air, she barely spared her a glance. All she could think of was the poor woman who had run out of time. *No more mistakes. No more dreams.* "That's terrible. Have they identified her?"

"She's a coed who attends one of the Houston schools. Do you realize what this means?"

Actually, she didn't have a clue. Nor did she approve of Judith's easy dismissal of the young victim. "Mrs.

Denton, please don't get me wrong, but I don't think—''

"He's uncontrollable now."

She couldn't keep up. "Who?"

"Your neighbor. *My* ex-husband."

"You can't be serious."

"Do you know where he was last night?"

Willa was tempted to tell her. Then she remembered that she couldn't speak for Zach's whereabouts earlier. She certainly wasn't going to admit that to Judith. But she also wasn't going to let Judith's announcement cloud her opinion of Zach.

"Mrs. Denton, I don't think—"

"We need to meet. Will you make time for me at three? Perhaps you can take a late lunch."

Under the circumstances, Willa didn't think she would find her appetite again today. Even if she could, Judith Denton was the last person she cared to share a meal with. "No, that won't be possible."

"This is for your own sake as well as some innocent victim's whose life you might help save. Don't turn me down."

The threat was unmistakable, the intent unforgivable. Even if she hadn't recognized what Judith was doing, Willa couldn't allow anyone to get away with such arrogance or manipulation. "I'll be here until closing, and I'm sure I can arrange to take a break if you stop by, but I hardly think discussing someone else's misfortune over a meal is anything either of us has in mind."

"You're right, of course" came the clipped reply. "Then I'll see you shortly."

Unbelievable, Willa thought, closing her eyes a moment to recuperate. And wouldn't Zach be upset if he knew what she had agreed to do. She had to be careful, of course. What he had accused his ex-wife of was beyond comprehensible. A woman like that couldn't be trusted. On the other hand, the mall was a public place and relatively safe; and Willa did need to find out what Judith was up to.

That poor, poor girl...

"Are you okay?"

Willa opened her eyes and smiled at Sophia, who'd come to ring up a gift basket of bath items. "Yes, thanks. But would you hold the fort for a moment? I need to go in the back and talk to Starla."

Stabbing her pencil into her bun, the black woman nodded. "Sure. It's still quiet. I'll sound the alarm if I need help."

After patting Sophia's shoulder in thanks, Willa went to her office where, as she'd suspected, her assistant was placing her purse in the file cabinet drawer they shared for that purpose.

"You can save the lecture," Starla said rather testily. "I had car trouble. It wasn't anything I could help."

Great, Willa thought, reaching over to her chair and into her tote bag for the newspaper she'd brought from home. This was what she needed—an attitude on top of everything else. So much for hoping that her friend had realized she'd made a mistake.

"I wasn't about to lecture, and I'm glad you're all right. Do you need time off to take care of repairs or anything?"

"It's taken care of."

Not the warmest of responses, but Willa decided to leave well enough alone. With an absent nod, she focused on the front page of the paper. While it wasn't a large paper by any stretch of the imagination, Vilary's was one of the few small-town papers that put out a

Sunday edition. What she read made her grateful that she hadn't seen this earlier.

"Oh my gosh!"

Starla must have seen her expression because she came to look over her shoulder. That answered one of Willa's questions.

"You didn't know, either?" The gratifying thing was that for an instant their personal problem seemed to have taken a back seat.

Starla shook her head. "I was so ticked off over my car that I didn't bother paying attention to anything but getting here. Linden Leahy..." She read the first paragraph aloud. "I don't think I know her."

Knew. Willa winced at the automatic correction. The name wasn't familiar to her, either, but she would guess anything that the girl had been a blue-eyed blonde. "Look—the police say she'd run out of gas and that her car was spotted late last night near here. That's what prompted such a quick search."

"Why on earth did he take her way over to your side of town?"

"I don't know, but it would seem he was someone who'd stopped to render aid."

"The wrong someone." Starla rubbed her bare arms. She was wearing a fuchsia linen shift today and an assortment of shell jewelry, which always earned her compliments from customers. But it often left her feeling chilly, even when there wasn't such frightening news. "Thank goodness one of my neighbors at the complex was around to help me out, or that could have been me."

"Was it that nice security guard you mentioned who lives below you?" Willa asked, hoping it might be. If Starla could get her mind off Ger Sacks...

"Uh-uh, it was what's his name. Elias. The guy from Lavender's."

She thought she'd had all the bad news she could handle for today, but she'd been wrong. Of all the names Starla could have mentioned, Willa didn't want to hear that one. And how did you ask the difficult questions without raising unwanted suspicions—or resentment? "Roger Elias...well. It's lucky you two were leaving at the same time, wasn't it?"

"Mmm. Did you know he'd been hurt? He has the nastiest bruise on his cheek. Kind of a scratch."

"That's too bad. How'd he get it?" Willa asked, hoping the question sounded casual.

"I have no idea. It would have been impolite to ask, wouldn't it?"

Having heard the first shadow of hostility returning to the younger woman's voice, Willa nodded. "No doubt you're right."

"But even though I used to think we had nothing in common, I'm considering giving him the benefit of the doubt."

"Meaning what?"

"Meaning that he asked me out, and I said yes."

As Starla tossed her braid over her shoulder and strode out of the office, Willa cast a final glance down at the paper and shook her head. Then she followed. "Starla, could I have a word with you?" Smiling at a customer who was headed back to the dressing rooms, she drew the taller woman back into her office. This time she shut the door.

"Please don't take this the wrong way," she began, holding up her hands when she saw the beginnings of a mutinous expression. "But are you sure this is a good time to start meeting new people? Taking into consideration what's going on around town…''

Starla crossed her arms and her Cupid's-bow mouth flattened with anger. "This isn't any of your business. I was merely making polite conversation, *not* asking for your permission."

Besides that, Willa had no room to talk when anyone could say the same thing to her about Zach. But in her case, *he'd* already done the warning.

"You're my friend. I care about you."

"Do you? Or could it be—now let me guess…" Starla tapped her chin and pretended to study the ceiling. "Why, don't tell me you're interested in him, too?"

That was uncalled for. Setting her hands on her hips, Willa demanded, "Say that again."

Although her confidence waned somewhat, Starla held her ground. "I think you heard me."

"Yes, but I'd hoped I was wrong, because you know what? That's two," she said, holding up her index and middle fingers. "For the sake of our friendship, don't push for number three. Now please relieve Sophia up front. She's going to unbox and set out some of the new loungewear that came in yesterday."

"It's my job to put out the new merchandise when you don't do it!"

"No," Willa said quietly. "It's a privilege I bestow on my friend. Since you're making it clear I may be wrong about our relationship, I have every right to choose any employee I care to."

And with that she opened the door in silent dismissal. Starla stalked out, and Willa shut it behind her. She needed a moment alone to soothe her nerves.

Oh, Zach. I hope you're having a better day than I am.

"May I come in, Mr. Denton?"

Zach pressed the remote control button to let Detective Pruitt enter, already knowing why the man was here. He'd read the paper shortly after Willa left. The news about the girl had left him shaken, and sorely tempted to telephone Willa at work just for the reassuring sound of her voice.

What a difference a day made.

He descended in the elevator and wheeled out to meet the weathered-looking cop, whose suit pants suggested that the man had done some searching near Cox Creek himself. "I know you can't accept a beer, but would you care for a soda, Detective? I believe there's something canned in the refrigerator. Bottled water, if you prefer."

If the man was surprised, he hid it well. "That's very hospitable of you. I'll take the water. It's been a hot day."

"In more ways that one," Zach murmured, leading the way to the kitchen. Too late he noted out of the corner of his eye the mess in the study. Pruitt didn't miss it, either.

"Little accident?"

"A mere fly in the ointment of life. I decided that even though men have been known to lose up to ten pounds during a chess tournament, it's an overrated game."

"Why's that?"

"Because although it's about mental acrobatics, the central piece, the one everyone's eye is on is the weakest. Virtually useless. A fraud. I'm talking about the king, Detective. The king is a *crawler*. We have that in common."

The cop cleared his throat. "Well, I don't know anything about the game, myself. I'm a poker man."

"Good for you. Instant gratification. I would imagine that for someone in your line of work that's a welcome change." Zach stopped before the refrigerator, aware he'd thrown his visitor off-balance. As he pulled open the door, he wondered what the cop would say about the concept that chess was also about offense, that without a loss of the opponent's balance, there could be no win. But he knew better than to share it. Pruitt was entertaining, but he was no fool.

"So you got a bit steamed over the game, did you?" the aging law-enforcement officer asked, murmuring his thanks as Zach handed him one of the glass bottles.

"Afraid so." Zach motioned to the old-fashioned opener screwed to the wall. "I thought I'd save you from having to ask the embarrassing question of whether or not I have a temper, Detective."

No hint of a smile eased the lines on the weary, gray-tinged face as Pruitt used the device. "Oh, I'm not shy, Mr. Denton. Were you playing alone?"

"Would you want someone witnessing your strike against futility, Detective?"

Nodding, the cop peered at the label before taking a long swallow, downing almost half the contents of the bottle, then uttered a belly-deep sigh. "That's very refreshing. It's amazing what they do to water these days, isn't it?"

He glanced around the kitchen and Zach knew he was taking mental notes: how the counters were virtually bare, the stove seemingly untouched—although Willa had cooked him a mouth-watering breakfast only hours ago—how the room, like the rest of the first floor appeared virtually uninhabited.

"You should see my wife's kitchen," Pruitt suddenly announced. "She collects salt-and-pepper shakers. There isn't an inch of space in our kitchen that isn't covered with the things. But you know what? Not one set has any salt or pepper in 'em. Says neither is good for me, so I have to collect what I can from the hot-to-go places and hide 'em in my pocket. People are funny creatures."

"I don't cook, and I don't have a maid," Zach replied, leading the cop closer to the point. The vibes he was suddenly getting from the detective weren't good. "If you need someone to verify my whereabouts at a certain time, I can't help you."

Pruitt looked down at him and beamed. "I wish everyone had your knack for catching on, Mr. Denton."

"Well, we all have our jobs to do. I have a publisher to appease, and I assume this isn't going to be your last call today."

"So you've read the paper?"

"Only a short time ago."

The cop watched bubbles rise in his mineral water. "It was a terrible thing. She was a such a pretty girl. Do you have any children?"

"I think you know I don't."

"Just refreshing my memory." Pruitt shook his head after giving Zach a sidelong glance. "No parent should have to live with the knowledge that their child's last moments were filled with terror and pain."

Zach remained silent, remembering his own so-called parents. To share that would be tantamount to putting a loaded gun to his head.

"On my way over here, I was trying to understand

how a person could do that to another person. There
was so much passion involved. It's different than war.
Were you in the service, Mr. Denton?''

"No."

"I was a marine in Nam."

Zach eyed the man's burr cut. "I would never have
guessed.''

"Ugly situation created by ugly men. Let politicians
run a war and you have a mess every time. Slaughter
is reduced to a job, soldiers are told to be dispassionate
machines. But what happened last night…it's different,
you know? Of course, you do," Pruitt said, snapping
his fingers. "It has to be similar to the way you write
your stories. Now there's some dark stuff…and look at
you—you don't seem like someone who'd go out and
do any of what you put in those books just so you can
make it real to your readers.''

"You've read my work, Detective?"

The man smoothed his out-of-fashion tie. "Well,
when you have a celebrity like yourself in a community
and folks are always discussing this book and that, it
makes you feel sort of funny not to be able to say you
have the thing at home, too.''

Zach was incapable of putting any amusement or
warmth into his smile. "Unlike some, I write to be read,
not simply to make a list and get a fatter royalty check,
Detective.''

"That's the first thing I noticed when I started reading your work. You're very passionate with your
prose—if that's the correct term? It's all personal to
you. You really take the reader inside a character's
mind, make him understand the reason a mind twists
and how a victim is chosen and feels. How do you do
it, Mr. Denton? How does a man like yourself so ob-

viously together create something that frightening and sick?"

"It's called imagination, Detective."

"Well, when they were handing it out, you were given yours *and* a few other people's share, I'll tell you that." Pruitt finished the rest of his drink. "You know what else impressed me? You're sneaky in choosing your victims."

"Sneaky?"

"Mmm. They appear randomly chosen—people in the wrong place at the wrong time and all that—and yet they fit a mold."

Zach swore silently as the detective carefully set the empty bottle on the counter. He could almost feel the room closing in around him, and he knew it would be foolish to pretend he didn't understand what the cop was driving at. "Are you saying that the young girl who was murdered last night fit the mold of the women that have been terrorized by the stalker, Detective?"

The older man shoved his hands into his trouser pockets and studied him for several seconds before murmuring, "Thank you again, Mr. Denton. Does it make you uneasy to know that someone may be styling his crimes after your methodology?"

"It's not a new concept," Zach said with a negligent shrug.

"No, sir, I'm not referring to the crimes themselves, rather the logic for choosing the victims."

Zach's stomach burned as if a stream of battery acid were dripping into it. "Then all I can say is that I pity you, Detective. I know I'm not reassured with the thought that there's two people walking this earth who have to deal with what goes on in my mind."

"I'm glad to hear you say that, Mr. Denton. And

feeling the way you do, you shouldn't mind telling me where you were last night between the hours of eleven and two.''

A droplet of sweat trickled down the back of Zach's neck into his T-shirt as he thought of the scream…of how Willa had been wandering outside for several minutes before entering his house…of that damned un-locked window. Had his instincts been off? What *would* have been different if he'd ignored his hunch and kept driving?

I wasn't supposed to come back. He knows I kept Willa with me. He killed the girl to punish me!

''Mr. Denton? Is something wrong?''

Only that he felt sick to his stomach. Again. And so damned helpless and manipulated.

''I've been fighting a virus,'' he murmured, using the excuse to massage his abdomen. ''And to answer your question, I was here. Why do you ask?''

''Because we found this near Linden Leahy's body.''

From his pocket Pruitt drew a small plastic bag. In-side was a slender piece of gold. It was a pin, maybe a tie tack. An expensive one of at least eighteen carats in the hard-to-miss shape of a fountain pen.

Zach wondered what showed on his face. If he re-flected anything close to the murderous emotions churn-ing inside him, he expected Pruitt to get the wrong idea and haul out his handcuffs at any moment. But the law-man would be wrong. The pin wasn't his…but he knew whom it belonged to.

''Yes, Detective?'' he asked, hoping that a lifted eye-brow offset his inner turmoil.

''It means nothing to you?''

''Why should it? Because it's a pen? I use a com-puter. And as you can see—'' he extended his arms to indicate his uniform of jeans and T-shirt ''—I've no reason to wear jewelry.''

''I understand,'' Pruitt murmured, as if filing this information away for later consideration. ''Most important, you didn't leave here at all last night?''

''Has someone suggested otherwise? Maybe I was seen rolling up and down the banks of Cox Creek? Did you find tracks from my chair, Detective Pruitt? Maybe you want to check for soil samples in the grooves of my tires?''

''Please, Mr. Denton, I didn't mean to agitate you. I just wanted to pass on that since the creek is so close to this area, we'll be doing house-to-house interviews. If I find out that you've been less than honest with me, I'll be extremely disappointed.''

CHAPTER SEVENTEEN

"I don't think you'll be disappointed," Willa said to the distinguished man before her. Once again she opened the sample bottle of the bath gel and held it up for him to smell. "It's not quite the ocean fragrance you preferred from the discontinued line but we've had a lovely response and I think your—" she glanced down noting again the fabulous emerald ring he wore on his left hand "—um, you'll find it extremely soothing after a stressful day."

"And it's all natural products like the other? My friend is so sensitive."

"She'll adore this. I've had women who can't go near other lotions swear by this one," she assured him, pointing to the splashes and creams in the set.

"Excellent. You've sold me."

Pleased, Willa carried the cellophane-wrapped basket to the register. She'd been concerned about losing this particular customer because, although he didn't come in often, when he did, cost wasn't a factor and he paid cash. In addition, he'd managed to keep her mind from—

The machine-gun staccato of high heels not only cut her off in midthought, it mocked her theory. Seconds later, Judith Denton's assertive, spicy, signature fragrance overpowered the store and the woman swept in. With her silver-and-yellow scarf flowing over one shoulder of a stunning matching silk suit, she made Willa feel gauche even in her beloved violet-blue coat-dress. "Sorry I'm late. I had an unexpected— Why, Felix! Imagine seeing you again...and here."

The man's expression didn't alter much, but he turned a pasty green; however, that's not what had Willa staring at him with surprise and wariness. The name Felix rang a sizable alarm inside her because Zach had mentioned a Felix!

This was his agent? She couldn't believe it. He'd been her customer for months! And what did Judith mean by "again"?

The telephone rang behind her. Wondering what else could go wrong, she glanced around hoping to get Starla or Sophia to take the call; however, both of them were tied up with customers.

"I'm so sorry," she said, gesturing helplessly. "Can you bear with me one moment?"

She introduced herself on the phone and began asking the caller to hold, only to be interrupted again.

"Willa!" a deep, familiar voice whispered urgently.

"Um...oh, yes. Hello, Mrs. King."

"Mrs.— You're not alone?"

"I can try to get that for you, ma'am, but could you hold on one second?" She glanced over her shoulder. "I'll be right with you both, sir, Mrs. Denton."

Zach sucked in a sharp breath. "Judith's there?"

"Actually there's two sizes in that line."

He hesitated. "Two. Wait a minute...the man you referred to as sir, is that it?"

"Right."

"You're telling me that I know him?"

"Well, in that line it's one of three, and I'm currently out. But my supplier is in Houston, so it shouldn't be long before that comes back in."

"Houston. Oh, my...*Fraser's in your store?*" A razor-sharp oath threatened to fray the phone line. "No wonder all I'm getting is his answering machine. What the hell's going on, Willa?"

"Could I call you back in a few minutes with that information, Mrs. King? We're terribly busy at the moment and I have people here waiting to check out. Would you like to give me your number?"

After dryly promising she would pay for her choice of names, he rattled it off to her. "And be careful about letting anyone see it."

She ripped the sheet of paper off the pad and tucked it into her pocket. "As soon as I'm able. Yes, I'll go back to my office, check the delivery date and give you a ring back."

"One more thing, sweetheart. Have you heard about the murder?"

Willa heard the anguish in his voice and her heart ached for him. "I'm afraid so, yes."

"You might be getting a visit from our friend Detective Pruitt. I should warn you that I told him I was home all night last night."

Had the policeman accused Zach of something? "I understand. I think."

"Just be careful with those two with you now. I mean it. Go nowhere with either one of them."

"No problem there. Goodbye, Mrs. King."

Her heart pounding, Willa again faced the two people waiting for her. "I must apologize again," she said, quickly resuming the sale to Zach's agent.

She wondered if her sudden unease showed as she worked. She felt shaky and all thumbs. It didn't help that while she'd been talking, she'd heard furious whispering going on behind her. Now Felix Fraser was glaring holes into her as if he knew who she'd been speaking with on the phone. For her part, Judith only appeared more confident, and calculating. In fact, her blue eyes made Willa recall Zach's chessboard. Particularly the cruel black queen.

After making change for Felix Fraser, she bagged his purchase in one of their prettier tote sacks and even added extra tissue paper, hoping it would appease the man. It didn't.

Ignoring her smile and words of thanks, he made a sharp, almost military pivot. With a withering glance toward Judith, he stalked out of the store.

"Nice to see you, Felix," Judith called after him. "Come and visit anytime." She laughed, a sound that held both mockery and amusement. "He's terribly choleric," she offered, turning back to Willa.

"I didn't realize you two knew each other." For her part, Willa wished the woman had left, too.

"Oh, Felix and I go way back." Several bangle bracelets jingled as the woman inspected a carousel of his-and-her key chains. "Did you know he's my husband's—" Again, the toxic laughter bubbled. "Oh, my. How silly of me. It must be these charming thingies reminding me of happier times. Zach and I used to have matching cars. But then the poor fool went out of his mind." She shot Willa a sidelong look. "*Did* you know about Felix?"

"Know what?"

The woman smiled, her poppy red lipstick creating a bold slash. "That he's Zach's agent, dear. What else?"

"No. I didn't," Willa said, knowing there was no reason why Judith shouldn't believe her. "How could I?"

"Indeed. How could you?" She ran a length of the scarf through her fingers, gazing at Willa over the rolled edge. Her eyes were truly a stunning blue, but held the warmth of a pit viper. "What does he generally buy? Bath products like those he picked up today?"

Willa decided the venomous creature had caused enough chaos. "Mrs. Denton, what can I do for you? As you can see, we're extremely busy today. I'm afraid I won't be able to leave the store after all."

Judith tapped her long nails on the counter. "It's imperative that we speak, *Mrs.* Whitney. I've come all the way down here on your behalf when I should be at the hospital at dear Nancy's bedside."

Dressed like that? Skeptical, but curious to know what the woman had up her sleeve, Willa gestured to the back of the store. "I could give you a minute in my office."

With a regal nod, Judith led the way.

After signaling Sophia, Willa followed. She didn't like the idea of taking Zach's ex-wife back there, not wanting her personal area poisoned with the woman's negativity. As it was, she would have to burn a fragrance candle in there afterward to purge the room of that cloying scent.

"All right, what's this about?" Willa asked, once they were inside and the door was closed.

"I think you're in danger."

Willa wasn't certain she'd heard Judith correctly. After all, the announcement had been issued while pacing the length of the room and inspecting everything as if she were in the market for an office herself.

Crossing her arms beneath her breasts, Willa leaned against the wall. "How so?"

The woman whirled around, her scarf rippling. Willa wondered if she practiced before a mirror.

"Don't be coy, dear. I saw the way you two exchanged glances last week when I was over there. And don't forget, I was married to the man." She resumed her pacing. "He can still be quite charismatic, even sensual, although his accident has done much to, er, affect his confidence sexually."

Incensed, it was all Willa could do not to grab Zach's ex-wife by the scruff of the neck and walk her out of the store. "That will be quite enough, Mrs. Denton."

Judith froze. "Excuse me?"

"Even if I had the time to do this, I wouldn't listen to gossip between or about a formerly married couple."

"You're trying to tell me that he hasn't spoken to you about me?"

"Fishing?"

The older woman retraced her steps, stopping only inches away from Willa. "You don't want to make an enemy of me, kiddo. And you don't want to come between me and what I want." She pointed toward the door. "That man took my love and the best years of my life and crushed them into the ground as thoroughly as he did that stupid plane of his. He made aspersions about my character in a court when he tried to divorce me and leave me without a dime. Me! After I worked beside him throughout our marriage to make him into the name he is today. Fortunately, I had justice on my side."

"And a good lawyer?"

The tortured, long-suffering expression vanished in a heartbeat. Judith narrowed her eyes. "You aren't all cotton candy, after all. But you're out of your league with me."

"Should I consider that a threat?"

"Only if you get in my way, dear." Judith smiled coldly. "Yes, I can see he's had enough clear moments to make quite an impression on you. So be it. But let me give you a piece of advice—when you're looking into his crazed gray eyes as he's squeezing the last breath from your lungs, don't forget that someone did try to warn you. And the tragedy is that it'll all be for nothing. You see, he won't be seeing you. His twisted mind will lead him to believe it's *me*."

"The Zachary Denton I've met wouldn't easily resort to violence," Willa replied, not caring if the woman ever set foot in Whimsy again or defamed her and her business to everyone else in town. "But I can see how someone like you would tempt him."

For a moment Willa wondered if she'd gone too far. Hatred radiated from Judith's eyes. Seeing the potential for all that Zach said his ex was capable of, it took considerable courage to reach for the door and stare her down.

"No one speaks to me like that," Judith whispered, slowly. "Ever."

"Goodbye, *Ms.* Denton."

Zach nearly went out of his mind waiting. *Come on,* he willed the telephone beside the computer. *Call!*

He couldn't believe this was happening to her. He was here, damn it. If anyone wanted a piece of him, let them come here! Why couldn't they leave her alone? The thought of Willa being in danger upset him so much that he told himself he would give her five more minutes. If she didn't call, he would drag himself out to the van and find out why not.

Never had he felt more impotent. Judith and Felix. It had been the least likely of the combinations, the one suspicion he'd wanted to be wrong about. But between what Pruitt had shown him, and Willa's news that they were together in her store, what other conclusion could he draw?

Finally the phone rang. He snatched it up before it had finished its first ring. "Yes!"

"I think I need that drink I poured you last night."

Never had he heard anything so wonderful as her voice. "Too late. I poured it and the rest of the bottle down the drain."

She hesitated. "I'm not sure I'm up for any more shocks today."

He was torn between chuckling with relief that she could still make jokes, and wanting to reach through the phone and hold her. "Was it bad? Are you okay? Tell me everything."

"I hardly know where to begin," she replied with a sigh. "The first thing I need to tell you is that Felix Fraser has been a customer of mine for quite a while, but I never knew who he was!"

"That's incredible." He didn't want to think of Willa having been exposed to him for all that time. It was bad enough to think the bastard had decided to do a little shopping after his night's activities.

"I would never have put it together because he always paid in cash and never offered the information. It was only when Judith walked in and called out to him that I discovered his name."

Zach frowned. "You mean they didn't come in together?"

"Oh, no. And he looked positively *ill* to see her. It happened just as you phoned. You wouldn't believe the harsh whispering that went on while you and I were talking."

"What happened after you hung up?"

"He paid for his merchandise, gave me a terrible look

and left. Judith taunted him, which didn't help. Why he put up with it I don't know. He always struck me as a no-nonsense, masterful sort. You know what he's like—he's your agent. But while Judith stood beside him, it was like watching a stranger. He appeared...well, terrified."

"That makes sense."

"It does?"

"Remember, I told you that the stalker loathed Judith as much as I do. Only later did the tone of the notes change."

"Yes, but Zach, she would have to have an incredible hold on him. Can you see Felix Fraser committing this horrendous crime last night and now shopping for bath products this afternoon? It's impossible to comprehend."

"That's because you're sane and have a conscience. But listen to this. Pruitt showed me a tie pin in the shape of a pen that they found near the murdered girl's body."

"What did he want you to do, break down and confess?"

"No doubt. He'd probably already shown it to Judith when he talked to her and I'm guessing she hinted strongly that it might be mine."

"That female is a— Zach, how *could* you have ever married someone like that?"

He grimaced. "I told you, I'm crazy."

"Humph. More likely, she's a remarkable actress."

"Just tell me that you didn't agree to anything she asked of you. I meant what I said, Willa. She's not to be trusted," Zach said, not wanting her to take Judith too lightly.

"Don't worry. I don't think she'll be bouncing checks at my place anymore. But finish telling me about this pin. What's it supposed to mean? Do you think it might belong to Felix?''

''I know it does. It's an antique, something he's had for years. But the best part is that when they clean it off in the lab, they're going to find he had his initials engraved on it. Once that breaks to the media, it'll only be a matter of time.''

''That's wonderful news! And it can't happen soon enough.''

He wanted to agree, but at that instant he looked out his window, just in time to see a car pull up before his house. ''No, it can't,'' he murmured instead. ''And I guess it won't.''

CHAPTER EIGHTEEN

"Zach? What's wrong? Zach!"

"Felix is here," Zach replied, his thoughts already racing to the possible ramifications of this unexpected visit. "I have to go."

"Don't let him in. Please? I'm calling the police!" Willa cried when he didn't respond to anything she'd said.

For his part, Zach felt amazingly calm. Eager for this meeting. "No. You forget, I'm prepared."

"He might be, too."

Somehow that didn't strike him as likely. "It wouldn't be his way. I'll call you back," he assured her gruffly. He was moved by her concern, tempted again to think of the future. Then the doorbell sounded and he hung up.

He listened to the sounds of the bolt releasing, the door opening and Felix's uncertain step.

"Zach?"

"Up here."

His agent chose the stairs, and his movements were slow. As if he carried a great burden, Zach thought, counting. When the tone of the steps told him Felix had arrived at the top and was headed down the hallway, he reached into his top drawer for the revolver and eased back the hammer.

"I should have called," Felix said, hesitant and drawn in the doorway. "But would you mind an impromptu visit? I've been driving around town all day trying to work up the courage to—''

''To what, you bastard?'' Zach asked, raising the gun.

If Felix had appeared terrified to Willa, he looked ready to pass out now. His skin matched the gray streaks in his hair, and since their last meeting he'd grown considerably gaunt. Vertical gashes on either side of his mouth running from eye to jaw made him look like one of the weather-ravaged carvings on Mount Rushmore. No longer did he resemble the shrewd and arrogant negotiator Zach had known, but simply an old broken man.

''Oh, God…Zach, don't,'' he moaned.

''Give me one good reason why I shouldn't.''

''I came to tell you myself. Isn't that worth something? For old times' sake?''

''Were you thinking of me when you were doing all that you did?''

''She was blackmailing me. I tried to think of a way out of it, but…I couldn't.''

''You damn well could have. You could have said no! It's not exactly missing from your vocabulary.''

''She's ruthless.''

''Not as ruthless as a jury is going to be.''

Felix closed his eyes as if in prayer. ''Please. I have money saved.''

''You think you can buy my silence?'' The man was more disgusting than imaginable. ''Wrong. You're going away, pal. And when they finally strap you to that table and stick that needle in your arm, I'm going to be there to applaud.''

Felix blinked, then frowned. ''What are you talking about?''

"Murder, you son of a bitch. Cold-blooded and premeditated murder. Two counts of it if that other woman doesn't make it."

"*What?*" The man wavered on his feet. "No! I didn't... You don't... I haven't killed anyone!"

"Tell that to the girl whose body is probably on some Austin forensic's table even as you stand there sweating into your silk suit."

"You think I did *that?*" Felix shook his head violently. "No. Oh, God, Zach, wait a minute. I may be guilty of some despicable things, of breaking your trust and cheating you. But rape and murder?"

"It's too late to deny it. The cops have the evidence to get a conviction. You're going down, pal."

Felix gripped the doorframe, clearly needing its support. "What evidence?"

"The gold pen you always wear?" Zach nodded to his agent's mauve-and-gray tie. "Didn't you even know you'd lost it? It was discovered near the girl's body. How long do you think it will take them to track you down once they find your initials on it? Then it'll just be a matter of matching sperm samples and..."

"The bitch!" Felix screamed, striking the doorframe with his fist. "The conniving, blackhearted— I'm being set up for this, Zach. I swear to you, I didn't do it." He laughed, his eyes frantic. "Look at me. Do I look like someone who's capable of such barbaric behavior?"

"That's the worst part of it," Zach admitted, although he kept the gun trained on his agent. "You were the one person I wanted to be wrong about."

"You *are* wrong. I did not kill anyone. I did not rape anyone." Felix raked his hand through his hair. "I don't know how my pin got where it did, okay? I have a strong hunch, but I am positive that I couldn't have lost it myself unless I rolled down my window while driving to or from here and literally threw it. And that didn't happen. You want to know why? Because I know where I did lose it. At Judith's.''

"So you admit to working with her?''

"With?'' Again the tall, agitated man shook his head. "No, no, no. Any contact we had was under duress. In fact I lost my pin the day I told you I was delivering her accounting report and check.''

"Really. Next you're going to tell me it came off when you two got into a wrestling match because the check wasn't big enough.''

"No,'' Felix returned with total levity, "we fought because I told her I was through ripping you off.''

Zach narrowed his eyes. "Explain that.''

Once again the look of shame had Felix avoiding his gaze. He leaned back against the frame and crossed his arms around his middle.

"She got hold of some damaging information and threatened to go public with it if I didn't make it worth her while to keep her mouth shut.''

"Damaging to whom?''

"Me!''

"And whose money did you use to pacify her?'' He watched the older man swallow and squirm. "Whose?''

"*Yours!*''

Zach had to rest his gun hand on the desk a moment because now he was shaking, shaking with fury. He didn't know why he felt worse; after all, a lost life was so many times more tragic than any amount of money. But this was a rape of a different sort, and yet another betrayal of trust.

"You mean above and beyond what the court

awarded her?'' he asked, so softly he barely heard himself.

Felix didn't nod this time; rather he lowered his head until his chin nearly rested on his chest.

''How much?''

''Over a hundred thousand.''

Impossible. He would have noticed it.

Granted, he'd been careless about a great many things and indifferent to even more, but he'd looked at the reports, damn it.

Yeah, doctored ones.

Zach could only think of one question to ask. ''Why?''

''I'd never have let her get away with it if there had been any way, Zach.''

''I don't give a damn what you think is a justifiable excuse,'' he growled, resentful that what little trust he possessed was being obliterated. ''Tell me what it is or I'll phone the police right now and you can explain yourself out of a murder charge.''

Felix covered his face with his hands and moaned pitifully before dropping them at his sides like a condemned man. ''She was in Houston about a year ago—at least that was the excuse she gave for stopping by. Maybe she'd been on to me all along. At any rate, I'm still in the dark as to how she found out where I live. But while I was on the phone, my roommate answered the door and there she was.''

''I don't get it. What? Did Judith later threaten to allude there was something between you two to break up you and your girlfriend?''

''No. She let me know that she'd seen me at a hotel restaurant earlier with my daughter.''

''*You* have a daughter?'' Zach gave himself a shake,

wondering what other revelations his so-called "friend" had been keeping from him. "When were you married?"

Felix rolled his eyes. "I wasn't. I had a wonderful but brief affair fifteen years ago. It was a difficult period for me and—it just happened. Anyway Kasey's mother was in Houston on a business trip and brought her along."

"Your roommate wouldn't be able to handle the news that you had a teenage daughter?"

"That was a blow, but hardly catastrophic. It was my daughter I needed to protect…and her mother. Karen is an attorney with an extremely conservative Philadelphia law firm. Neither she, nor Kasey who goes to an exclusive private school, would be able to handle the fact that I now live with another man."

Zach pinched the bridge of his nose. No wonder Judith had followed him like a bloodhound. She'd always been a soap opera addict; this was right up her alley!

Silence stretched until Felix pleaded, "Say something, will you? Or better yet, do me a favor and use that damned gun."

Instead, Zach eased the hammer back into its safety position and replied, "You steal from me. You lie to me. You get yourself in such a mess that you're blackmailed by the woman you *know* tried to kill me, and you want me to do you a favor and put you out of your misery?" He opened the drawer and put away the gun. "Oh, no, pal. It doesn't work like that."

"But what am I going to do?" Felix cried, stepping farther into the room now that the gun was out of sight.

"You're going to release me from our contract for one thing."

"You don't have to ask for that because it'll be automatic once I'm in prison, which is where I'm sure to end up, thanks to what Judith's done.''

The idea should have brought pleasure and didn't. Annoyed, Zach muttered, "I'd rather not wait. And you'd better get with your attorney and draft a statement of intent to pay me back before your daughter's mother decides to sue you for injury, as well."

"Anything, Zach. Whatever you say. Consider it done."

"I'll believe that when I have my money back," he replied coldly, his mind already shifting to other things.

He wondered how many people Judith was manipulating and blackmailing. No one could keep up her reckless, ruthless pace without running out of luck; in fact, he was amazed someone hadn't taken revenge already. Unfortunately, he couldn't wait for that, or for the law to do him a favor. Too many lives were still at risk—especially Willa's.

At least there was an ounce of good news in all of this. Whether she'd intended to or not, Judith had taken some of the pressure off him as being a suspect in the murder of the Leahy girl. And now his own list of suspects were narrowed down to two.

He had to find out whether Ger Sacks or Roger Elias was the stalker before he struck again. And an idea came to mind.

"Did you ever see anyone else around her place when you went by Judith's?"

"No. No one except her cleaning woman."

"No unexpected guest? There wasn't someone you glimpsed in another room?"

"I always phoned ahead of time to let her know I was coming—you know what a flitter she is—and even then I'd often have to wait in my car until she arrived from who knows where. Why? Is there another problem?''

Just one, but so deadly that it made what Felix had done seem trivial in comparison, Zach thought, missing his Scotch for the first time today. And Roger Elias was due in a matter of hours for their Sunday game. Under the circumstances, he really needed to turn up the heat tonight. It was obvious the pressure was getting to Judith's puppet; could he add to it without causing another young woman to be hurt? He needed to think. Preparations had to be made, and most of all Willa needed to be warned to keep her distance just in case.

Felix cleared his throat. ''Is there anything else I can do, Zach?''

He looked relieved, even hopeful, that this was off his chest. Zach stared at the man, realizing that in a few weeks Felix would have come to terms with this whole episode. In a few months he might even have turned it around so that it was his client's fault for bringing Judith into their lives in the first place.

No, this was nothing compared to a life. But it demanded a price. ''Yes,'' he replied his look holding closure. ''You can get out of my house.''

CHAPTER NINETEEN

As soon as he'd locked the door behind Felix, Zach began to telephone Willa. He stopped himself just as quickly. Aware of the anger and bitterness still seething inside him, and not wanting to expose her to any more of it than necessary, even if she was anxiously awaiting a call, he decided to first go downstairs and clean up the mess in the study.

He liked the protectiveness and generosity in that impulse, despite the sharp little voice beneath it that mocked him. *After so much time alone, is it the woman you're reacting to, or simply the craving for human contact?* But he knew that voice. It was the same one that had told him he could never write a book, then finish it, then sell it. Muttering, "Take a hike," he wheeled himself to the elevator and lowered the car to the first floor.

Lifting the table meant easing himself to the floor and using his considerable arm and torso strength. But since he had to crawl around to locate all the game pieces anyway, it was hardly an inconvenience. It did trigger a flood of memories, though, reminding him of how dark his spirit had been when he'd first spotted Willa on the floor and believed the worst; of how brutal and painful her bruises had been; of the incredible night they'd shared.

He wanted her again. Now. In a hair-trigger response, his body heated and tightened. When he found the white queen, he closed his fingers tightly around it, and leaned back against a chair to savor the feeling, the memories...how quickly she was becoming his sanity.

God, you're developing a case.

"Can schizophrenia be far behind?" he drawled, reaching for his metal chariot. No sooner did he settle himself back in the chair, than the phone began ringing. He smiled wryly. No doubt Willa had felt the power of his thoughts and hadn't been able to wait any longer for him to call.

"Don't worry, I'm still alive," he murmured into the mouthpiece.

After a brief pause a dry male voice replied, "I'm glad to hear that, man."

Ger? This was definitely unexpected. He had to do some fast thinking to cover his blunder.

"Hell, I thought you were my agent again. He's been checking on me ever since the news about the murder broke."

His trainer grunted something, adding, "Yeah, everyone's been dragging around here all day. Seems the girl was a member for a while. I don't remember her, but a bunch of the others do. That's why I'm calling. Everybody must either be depressed or scared, and business is a real bummer. So I was wondering if you felt like taking an extra workout today?"

Another guy with the soul of a slug, Zach thought drolly. Did he think women cared about their thighs and men about their beer bellies at a time like this? Only the fact that his focus was intensifying on Ger kept Zach from telling him to get a life.

"Sounds okay. What time?"

"How about— Can you hold on a second?"

Zach listened as Ger turned away to respond to someone who'd interrupted. He had to concentrate because it sounded as if Ger had the receiver either pressed to his chest or almost covered with his hand. Still Zach faintly heard the man swear and say something like *"—her. She can't do this to me!"* The person bearing the bad news made a brief comment to that and a second later Ger replied, *"All right. All right! Tell her I'm coming."*

Then to Zach he said, "Ah…sorry, man. This real pain in the— I just learned another customer needs me. I have to cancel out."

Damn. Zach did some quick calculating. "How about later? I'm available until around seven." He figured that would give him time enough to shower and prepare for Elias.

"Better not. I never know, uh…forget it. I can't," he muttered, sounding more rattled by the minute. "Sorry I bugged you."

Zach sat listening to empty air space for several seconds before he hung up. Who was the customer who'd flustered the trainer so? Was he indulging in too much wishful thinking, or had Judith gotten a message through to her puppet? The timing was right. After that exchange with Felix in Willa's store, Judith would be foaming at the mouth. It fit…it fit…but could he be sure?

Returning to the study, he finished resetting the chess pieces. Then he hurried back upstairs, knowing Willa would be getting frantic.

As he picked up the phone, he realized he had no dial tone. "Sweetheart? Is that you?"

"This is Roger. Roger Elias. Guess my timing's off. It sounds as if you're expecting another call."

Zach shut his eyes, tempted to beat his head against the desk. Now what? he wondered.

"It's no problem, Roger. What's up?"

"I can't come tonight."

The words came out in a rush, and sounded tense, leaving Zach with the impression that he didn't want to explain himself, either. "Is there something wrong?"

"No, I… Something's come up and I won't be able to make it, that's all."

But in all the time they'd been meeting, he'd only missed one night and that was last winter when an ice storm had raged through most of Texas. It struck Zach as highly coincidental that Elias should choose tonight for his second absence.

"I see," he said simply, aware of silence's power on the psyche, particularly on the telephone. He hoped that would make Elias squirm enough to slip up and provide some piece of information. Zach knew he couldn't afford to wait until their next game.

"It's not a problem, is it? You, er, sounded like you might have something lined up anyway."

That's the one thing Zach didn't want him to suspect. "Oh, *that.* I'd been cut off from my agent's assistant, and I thought she was calling back."

"Oh. I thought…since you said 'sweetheart'…"

"If you heard her voice, you'd understand. She sounds twenty minutes out of college. Blonde. Blue-eyed. Anyway," he added quickly, before Roger tried to cut him off, "I'll miss the game. You do give the day a boost when I have to anticipate whether you'll challenge me with either a Catalan Opening, or the Latvian Gambit or the Slav Defense."

"You don't have to say that because you think it'll make me feel better. I thought you might be glad for the break. I seem to be getting on your nerves lately, anyway."

Zach's gut instinct was to keep pacifying the younger man. He'd dropped enough hints to make it clear he knew who he was talking to—or thought he knew. As much as he loathed empty gestures and insincere compliments, he would do that and more if it meant keeping the stalker from striking again. He had to remember the man had been drawn to him first because of hero worship.

"Nothing could be further from the truth, Roger. Apparently, I've let my work and my self-destructive habits get the best of me, and at expense to you. I apologize."

"I *hate* it when you patronize me."

The slam of the phone forced Zach to jerk the receiver away from his ear. *What the hell...?* And he thought he'd been losing his mind?

He hung up the receiver, but didn't take his hand away. Willa wasn't going to believe this, he thought, glancing down at the number he'd written down. He dialed her number.

The moment he heard her voice, he murmured, "I wish it was closing time."

"What on earth took you so long? I didn't take nearly as long as you did!"

"You didn't have three different maniacs to deal with."

That quieted her. "What do you mean? I'm in my office—it's okay."

First he told her about Felix—a summarized version, but she seemed to get the idea. What helped him most was that, as he'd learned last night, she was a good listener, and cared.

"Zach, bless your heart," she whispered when he'd finished sharing the first part of his story. "I can't believe he did that to you! Are you all right? Did you mean what you said when I answered the phone? Let me make a few calls to bring in more staff. I can be there in…a half hour?''

"Hey, that was just self-pity talking. You have enough on your hands.'' But he was moved by her gesture. It had been a long time since anyone had offered to make such a sacrifice for him. "I'll survive—if you'll promise to let me see you later.''

Her sigh barely made it across the line. "I'm so glad you want to.''

"Willa, I'd push the sun down and drag up the moon if I could,'' he confessed, a little embarrassed at how eager that made him sound.

"I'd help you if *I* could,'' she whispered back. Then she grew sad and angry. "Blast it all! He seemed like such a dignified, honest man. I liked him, Zach. Yes, he was a bit rigid and formal, but I thought that was just a part of his commitment to excellence. Instead he's the world's worst waffler! No wonder Judith took such pleasure taking cat swipes at him. Surely he can't believe she'll leave him alone now?''

Zach had wondered about the same thing. "I suppose he thinks if he doesn't have access to my money, he's no longer worth harassing, but you're right. That's naive on his part and shows he still doesn't know what he's dealing with. He thinks he's dealing with a witch, when in actuality he has someone far more dangerous on his hands.''

"If only he would go to the police!''

"Felix? Unlikely,'' Zach said, with a new understanding of the man. "He's the type to push to the limit for a client because it's abstract and never really touches him personally. But personally, he's an emotional coward.''

''At least you have to give him some credit for trying to protect his daughter and the girl's mother.''

Zach tried with only minor success. ''I'd feel more generous if I believed they were his chief concern. But I'm not convinced it isn't his living arrangement he's more interested in protecting.''

''I was afraid you might say that.'' Willa took a deep, emotion-settling breath. ''Well, that certainly narrows your list, doesn't it?''

''In a way. But listen to what happened next and tell me it's not getting more complicated.'' He then shared his experience with Ger and Roger's strange phone calls.

''Good grief!'' she groaned when he was done. ''I thought I'd been put through fire, but you have two volcanoes that sound as if they're about to explode in your face.''

The analogy was frighteningly on target. ''The damnedest thing is that I haven't received any more notes. What's up? Why the sudden reticence?''

''He may be watching to see how you react. Or maybe Judith has forbidden him from doing any more?'' Willa suggested, sounding just as mystified. ''What if the murder was unexpected to her, as well?''

Zach frowned. ''What do you mean?''

''I know it's dangerous to play doctor, but it sounds as if we're dealing with two psychotic personalities. Maybe she tugged on the wrong line and is finding out that her puppet isn't as controllable as she'd thought.''

''There's nightmare,'' Zach murmured, although he was impressed with her logic.

''The thing is that I can easily check on Ger's story

to you. I only have to go next door under the pretense of having lost something yesterday.''

"No way!''

"But if he's there, at least we'd know he was probably placating one of the club's clients. He's an indiscriminating flirt, Zach, and it's possible that he's spread his favors too thin. Maybe that interchange you overheard was some sugar mama getting testy.''

"Judith doesn't share. Anything.'' This was a given Zach told himself he couldn't forget. In keeping with the old expression about cutting off one's nose to spite the face, she would destroy everything before yielding or surrendering. Knowing how frighteningly intense, he must have sounded, he quickly added, "At any rate, you can't assume he won't see through your ploy. Besides, Roger may be the one I should be focusing on anyway.''

Willa made a pained sound. "He's too…wimpy, Zach.''

"There's a great deal of anger inside him.''

"He's nowhere as physically dominating as Ger Sacks.''

"But he has his own leverage, namely his harmless appearance,'' Zach insisted, having dealt with all her arguments himself. "Who would you be more likely to turn your back on, Ger or Roger?''

"Oh, damn.''

When she didn't say anything else for several seconds, he frowned and asked, "What is it?''

"He's asked my assistant manager out.''

"I thought she was after Sacks?'' he replied, confused.

"She's after *love*.''

Zach finally understood. He'd made the mistake himself. Once. "You have to stop her."

"You think she's listening to me after last night? And things are even worse now. I'm not even sure I'll be able to keep her as an employee."

"Stop her, Willa. We're talking about her life."

"She's not a blonde and she doesn't have blue eyes," she ground out, her concern and fear apparent.

Zach was careful to keep his voice gentle. "And what if that's no longer a criteria?"

"Then I have to tell her."

"Short of that."

"Zach, there's no other way she'll believe me!"

He knew that. But he also knew that the more people who they confided in, the weaker his control of events. *Who are you kidding? You haven't had control since the notes changed.*

He exhaled, knowing he, too, had a major decision to make. "All right. Tell her. And I'll phone Pruitt."

"You mean you're going to show him the notes?" Willa asked, concerned.

"More than that. I'm going to tell him everything."

"Oh, Zach…there has to be another way. He'll charge you with complicity!"

"Maybe. Interfering and hampering for certain." But he had no choice. He saw now that he'd run out of options, at least from a moral standpoint. He wouldn't risk any further attacks; nor would he put Willa through the emotional trauma of knowing she could have kept a person she cared for from being hurt. "It has to be done."

"At least wait for me."

"Sweetheart, Pruitt's going to be ticked off as it is.

Do you think he's going to be in a better frame of mind if I wait until the middle of the night to call him?"

"At least give me an hour. As soon as I hang up, I'll bring Starla into my office and explain things to her," Willa entreated urgently. "If she comes around, I can leave her in charge of the store and be with you by...five? Zach, my input is important, too."

She was trying to protect him. Again. And knowing she would do what she wanted regardless, Zach relented, adding, "I don't deserve this—or you."

"Great," she replied softly. "Now that we both might be heading for jail, you start sweet-talking me." Then she hung up, as if she knew what response he would make to that.

The first thing Willa did when she ended her call with Zach was to telephone for more sales help. It took her three calls, but she found the woman she wanted to offset her absence.

Immediately afterward, she signaled Starla into her office. The younger woman's resentful expression wasn't reassuring as she strode in and dropped into the chair beside the desk, but Willa hoped that once she began listening, things might change.

"Why didn't you tell me?" Starla groaned, pressing her hands to her cheeks. The pink matched the intense shade of her dress. "And all this time I thought..."

Seeing her guilty glance, Willa managed a wry smile. "I know what you thought. And I won't say I wasn't offended by it because I thought we had a better basis of trust than that. But what's important now is that you don't get hurt, and I help Zach get through this."

"You're really taking a gamble by telling me all

this,'' Starla murmured, shaking her head in wonder. "I haven't earned the faith, but thank you.''

"You're welcome.''

"You're really getting serious about him, aren't you?''

Willa shoved her hands into her pockets and tucked her head like a turtle. "I didn't want to. I *don't* want to. Good grief, I'm not ready for this—I've just bought a house, I have this place that takes up so much of my time and he's had such a terrible life, who knows if he can even think beyond one day at a time. But…'' She shrugged out of the tense pose. "It's happened and we're going to have to deal with it.''

"I know that tactic.'' Starla nodded with confidence, the warmth returning to her eyes. "The more defined and logical you get when describing your feelings, the more you care.'' She rose, clenching and unclenching her hands as if not knowing what to do with them. "And I'm a twit. Roger Elias and Ger Sacks…do I pick 'em or what? Jeez, maybe I need a therapist.''

Willa hugged her, knowing Starla was too burdened with guilt to initiate the gesture herself. "Maybe you need to stop trying so hard. I think if you concentrate on being yourself, the real you, then the rest of your life will fall into place.''

"Maybe I'd like to talk to you about that sometime.'' Blinking, Starla backed away and offered a shy smile. "You get moving.''

"What about your date with Roger?''

"I'll call and let him know I have to work. Don't worry. We'll be okay here.''

This was the Starla she'd thought she'd lost. Sighing with relief, Willa touched the younger woman's arm, then grabbed up her purse.

CHAPTER TWENTY

Willa could tell that Detective Pruitt wasn't pleased when he saw her and Zach together. He arrived only minutes after Zach called him—which Zach had done only after drawing her close for a long, achingly sweet kiss. Willa had let the policeman into the house, leading him to the study, where she'd stopped beside Zach, placing her hand on his shoulder.

"Why do I know I'm about to be greatly disappointed?" he asked, looking from one of them to the other.

Zach motioned to the chess table where the board was pushed aside to make room for several items. "Maybe you'll want to look at those before I make my statement. The one on top of the purported evidence taken from Nancy Porter was left in Mrs. Whitney's mailbox the day before she moved in next door. I would wager only hours before Ms. Porter was attacked. The notes on the right are those I've been receiving for several weeks."

The lawman pressed his lips together and, with a negative move of his head, approached the table. After glancing at her note, Willa watched him lift it and see the red panties she'd put in the freezer bag. The look he shot her over his shoulder had Zach laying his hand over hers.

"I don't believe they were part of the set Ms. Denton referred to," Willa began, although her voice sounded thin at first. "A few days after the incident, I made myself examine them more closely, and I recognized that the manufacturer isn't the same one who does the set Ms. Porter was supposed to be wearing.''

"That doesn't excuse what you did. It's our job to determine what is and isn't relative.'' Detective Pruitt gestured to the note. "Didn't this frighten you? You weren't inclined to notify the police?''

"She thought I'd put it in her mailbox,'' Zach interjected before she could reply. He tightened his hold of her hand. "It arrived after we'd had a brief but...unpromising introduction.''

"Must have been some meeting.'' The aging policeman shifted slightly and took up the handful of notes Zach had received. He spent almost a full minute going through them. "All right, Mr. Denton, I'll ask you the same question. This is disturbing no matter how you tried to look at it. You felt no need to notify us?''

"You read what he said in the fourth one, Detective. If I went to the police, someone would pay. Perhaps you should hear my story first,'' Zach told him, calmly. "That may resolve some of the mystery and nullify most of the questions.''

"Go on, Mr. Denton. But I should warn you that you have a right to have an attorney present. You and Mrs. Whitney both.''

Willa intercepted Zach's glance and smiled to reassure him, and let him know she had every confidence in him. As their gazes clung, she once again felt that mysterious but wonderful aura, as if they were the only ones in the room.

When Detective Pruitt cleared his throat, Zach turned back to their visitor. "We have no problem sharing what we have to say with you, Detective.''

"Then by all means, proceed.''

Zach told his story, not as a writer trying to grip an

audience, or as a public speaker intent on swaying the listener's position one way or another; he simply conversed as if they were two acquaintances sitting across from each other at a bar catching up on the last several years of news. It was easy in delivery if not content, and yet wholly without embellishment. Willa found herself moved again, even though she was hearing some parts for the second time in only days.

But what did Jack Pruitt think? That was hard to determine, for if Zach was a good speaker, then the experienced policeman was an excellent listener. Tugging down his tie and releasing the top button on his suit shirt, he simply shoved his hands into his pants pockets, pursed his generous lips and scowled. He reminded Willa of Long John Silver in *Treasure Island,* and that amusing thought wasn't altogether reassuring. Did the wily detective mean to look comical as a means to disarm them?

If so, it didn't work on Zach. He kept to the facts, answered questions when they were volleyed at him, and when he was through, he didn't grasp for anything to fill the silence; he simply waited for Detective Pruitt to respond however he would.

The police officer nodded several times as he considered the material on the table. Or was it the chess pieces themselves? Willa wondered.

"Greed and revenge," he murmured at last. "Why is it that so much of a cop's work is tied up with those two…?"

"Cancers?" Zach offered. "Because 'a man that studieth revenge keeps his own wounds green.' Bacon," he supplied at Pruitt's questioning look. "Who, when it came to greed and ambition, by the way, didn't escape some condemnation himself."

Detective Pruitt's grunt held disdain. "For someone so danged smart, you've made a nice mess for yourself, my friend. Still…your story is just ridiculous and sick enough to be true."

"You can verify Judith's threats before the plane crash and her behavior since with my agent. My ex-agent," Zach corrected when the policeman lifted an eyebrow. "And he'll confirm her blackmailing scheme, which led him to embezzle money from me. That will explain how his tie pin ended up at the murder site. It's up to him whether he wants to disclose the reasons for the blackmail, though I have no doubt Judith will have no reservations in sharing the information with anyone who'll listen."

"She'll also say that you had more of a reason to frame Fraser than she did."

"She'll be wrong because to know me is to know it's enough that Felix pays me back and never makes another penny off me again. You see," he added with a frosty smile, "he and Judith have a love of money in common. It will drive him crazy if I become even more successful without him. And, believe me, I have plenty of dark corners to explore on paper.

"In the same vein, Judith was wrong when she chose to have either Elias or Sacks leave the pin after the murder. First, it detracted from her allegations that I was the stalker. Second, only an idiot would use someone so easily connected to them if they were masterminding the crimes."

"Yet you've been hiding the fact that you can walk," the detective pointed out. "Or does Gerald Sacks know?"

"He knows I have some feeling, and that I have considerable pain at times due to nerve damage, but I've been careful to let him assume that they won't hold my weight. Actually, they barely will without the assistance of my canes."

Detective Pruitt scratched his furrowed forehead. "And you think Ms. Denton set up her own houseguest as the first victim?"

"Maybe I can provide some insight there," Willa told him. She then shared her earlier experience with Judith in her shop, the woman's history of writing hot checks and, finally, her threat.

Her comments did seem to make an impression with the detective. "I'll admit I have seen her behavior take sudden turns as you described," he murmured, as though thinking out loud. "On the other hand, one could say that you might have a motive for damaging Ms. Denton's reputation, since you and Mr. Denton seem to be, er, so close."

Willa could feel Zach stiffen. She tried to restrain him, but he gently extricated himself from her hold and wheeled himself closer to the detective.

"Willa *is* the woman mentioned in those notes as the stalker's ultimate target, make no mistake, Detective. And why? Because she happened to be born beautiful, blond and blue-eyed. But even more, because she's a caring, generous human being who either Sacks or Elias *and* Judith knew would shatter the emotional walls I've worked hard to build around myself. I resent your implication that she's somehow to blame for anything. If anyone deserves to be accused, it's me for subjecting her to danger!"

"Zach, it's all right." Willa crouched beside him and touched her forehead to his upper arm, hurting for him, and at the same time overwhelmed with his declaration. Did he realize how much he'd almost confessed?

He clasped her fingers with his left hand and stroked her hair with his right. Except for when they'd made love, she'd never felt him shake so. She couldn't bear what this was doing to him.

"Detective," she said, looking up at the older man, "tell us what we need to do to make this insanity stop."

He drew out one of the chairs at the table, sat and took out a notebook. "I'll follow up on everything you've given me. Hopefully, something will give us the break we need. Care to tell me your hunches on which of these two is our stalker?"

"Ger Sacks," Willa said.

"Roger Elias," Zach said at the same time.

They exchanged glances and Willa knew they'd just given Detective Pruitt one more thing to doubt about them.

"Which of the men have you had the most contact with?" the police officer asked her.

She thought about it and shook her head. "Well, neither. I know them both by sight and name, and we've exchanged the bare minimum of words, but..."

"Why don't we go over a few things one more time," the lawman said, wearily, clicking his pen. "I want to make sure I have everything straight."

Almost an hour later, Detective Pruitt finally headed toward the door, the notes and bag in hand. "I don't suppose I have to warn you not to leave town?"

Her spirits sinking, Willa forced herself to ask, "Does that mean we should call an attorney?" Lord, what was she going to tell her family? And how was an arrest on her record going to affect her business?

"Not quite yet," he replied, the hint of warmth in his eyes. "Are you going back to the store tonight?"

"No," Zach said before she could answer.

Willa didn't dare meet his gaze. "I guess I can get my assistant to lock up for me," she told the policeman. But her thoughts were all on Zach. Drat the man, she moaned, he was determined to make her blush yet.

Detective Pruitt opened the door. "All right, then I'll have the night shift make sure they keep an eye out on your street. And if something comes up, here's my home number." He handed her a business card.

She hated that her hand wasn't quite steady as she accepted it. If he hadn't mentioned the patrol, she would have been fine.

"And don't go wandering around outside, okay?"

Her tension eased. She even managed to smile back at him. "Yes, sir. I promise. Thank you, Detective."

She closed and locked the door behind him. "I think it's going to be all right," she murmured turning, only to find Zach watching her with an intensity she was beginning to recognize all too well. She leaned back against the door. "What?"

"Now all you have to do is worry about the danger in here."

CHAPTER TWENTY-ONE

Willa wondered if there was another man alive, other than Zach Denton, who knew how to make a lady feel both priceless and in trouble. As she slipped the business card into her breast pocket, she shook her head. "You know I should go back. Starla took things extremely well, and I think we're going to be okay again, but I should go back."

"You heard Pruitt."

"We have mall security. The guard could walk me to my car after we close. Then it would only be— Zach, I can't think straight when you look at me like that."

"I don't want you to think straight. It's been a long hellacious day for both of us, and I'm tired of probing questions, and threats and nightmares.... Come upstairs with me."

Four little words and he started the fever in her all over again. "Let me at least call the store?"

"Call. Then come upstairs."

By the time she reached the phone, punched in the numbers and glanced over her shoulder, he was gone. Seconds later she heard the elevator rising. Watching the car go up, she shook her head in bemusement, wondering if it was eagerness or his desire to give her privacy that had made him go.

Her conversation with Starla took several minutes. Her assistant reassured her that everything was fine at the store, that, of course, they could lock up without "the boss." More interested in the meeting with Detective Pruitt, the younger woman asked countless questions. As for canceling her date with Roger, she sounded frustrated by the man's lack of reaction.

"He just said 'I see' and hung up on me," she reported, exasperated. "If he thinks I'm lying about having to work, all he has to do is walk down this way and see I'm still here."

For her part, Willa didn't like his reaction at all. She had Starla promise to ask one of the guards on night shift to be sure to keep an eye on all the staff as they left the building. "And see that he's nearby when you go to your car, too. Promise?"

Not only did her assistant comply, but she added that she would be spending the night at her parents' house. She explained that she'd already been in touch with them and they would be expecting her. "I just don't feel comfortable going back to the apartment alone, knowing he's headed there, too."

Much relieved, Willa gave her Zach's number, warning her not to share it with anyone, and also Detective Pruitt's at home, in case of an emergency. She ended the call a short time later, confident that she couldn't have done more if she was at the store herself.

As she climbed the stairs, she drew out the pins holding her long hair in a French twist, only then realizing how the formal style had been adding to the tension building at the base of her neck. It felt wonderful to shake her hair free, and she was smiling as she reached the doorway of Zach's bedroom.

"Stop there."

Already in bed, he sat against the pillows and headboard, the sheet pulled up to his hips. The welcome in his eyes and the intent sent a tingling warmth through her body.

"What?" she asked softly.

"I just want to look at you."

"What a coincidence." For him, she combed her fingers through her hair, lifting it off her shoulders before shaking it into a less tame style. "I like to look at you, too."

"The call go okay?"

"Everything's fine." She removed the waist-length strand of gold and pearls, laying it and the pins on the counter to her left. Suddenly she realized that neither of them had eaten in hours. "Hungry?"

"Starved."

"Want me to make us something?"

"Later. Unbutton the dress."

She did, slowly. Then she let it hang open, knowing he could catch glimpses of the matching lingerie she wore beneath as she released the fastenings on her cuffs. When she finished, she eased the dress off her shoulders, slipped it down her arms and laid it neatly over the chair on her right.

With a smile tugging at her mouth, she murmured, "More?"

He sighed. "That would be nice."

Next, she hooked her thumbs into the elastic waist of her half-slip and pushed it over her hips. She bent at the waist, knowing it would give him an optimum view of her lace demibra, and as the slip puddled around her feet, she stepped out of the satin ring and gracefully picked it up.

"Pretty, isn't it?" she murmured, setting the garment over the dress.

"Pretty lethal. Would you mind turning around?"

Laughing throatily, she did a slow pirouette, knowing what it would do to him to see the minimum of lace that made up her briefs and the garter that held up her lace-edged stockings. He'd opened the drapes on her left just enough for the afternoon light to peek through the sheers and illuminate her fair skin and the rich blue hues in her lingerie. "Okay?"

He shook his head. "I think you'd better come here."

She let the pull of his gaze draw her, stepping out of her heels in the last second before kneeling on the bed. Tossing her hair over one shoulder, she approached him on all fours like a stalking cat. She understood what he wanted, the escape and release from the darkness and fears that constantly pulled him into the shadows. He needed play. Fantasy.

"What seems to be the problem?" she purred.

"You. You were too far away."

"Is this better?" she asked, straddling him, but staying up on her knees.

"Much." He hooked an arm around her waist and buried his face between her breasts, only to moan as he nuzzled her. "How can you smell more delicious than you look?"

"All you're smelling is me and vanilla cream soap."

"Must be the combination." He traced the décolletage of her bra with his lips. "Because until now I never had this craving for sweets."

"Interesting. Still—" she moistened her lips as his breath seared through the lace and made her nipple tauten and ache "—you don't want to draw any hasty conclusions."

"You're right. I should take my time and make sure."

He did, opening his mouth over her, while he cupped and caressed her with his hand. Willa watched, finding that it was as seductive as feeling, to see the contrast

of his romantically dark hair teasing her pale skin, the
working of the muscles in his cheeks as he explored
and caressed her, his strong fingers restless yet worshiping. As he bestowed the same attention on her other
breast, he released the front closure of her bra. Willa
leaned closer, slid her fingers into his hair and stroked
her pelvis against his muscular chest.

She smiled, not surprised at the deep-throated rumble
that rose in his throat, and arched back when he began
trailing a path of steamy kisses and love bites down her
body. He encouraged her by shifting his hold to her
hips. Bent like a bow, she felt her bra slip down her
arms, then sighed as he slowly released the first garter
and suspensefully moved on to the other three.

"Whispers," he murmured against her taut body.

"Hmm?"

"I'd forgotten the wonderful sounds between a man
and woman. The whispers of lace against cotton…male
skin against female skin…metal against metal," he
added smiling as he slipped hooks from eyes and finally
removed the garter belt. Tossing it aside, he suddenly
rolled her beneath him. "Do you hear it? Perfect or-
chestral synergy. Listen."

He drew his hand down her body igniting a current
of awareness that made her breath catch when he
reached the lace between her thighs.

"That's the most beautiful sound of all. Your pleasure."

With his back to the only light entering the shadow-
filled room, he looked threatening, invincible as he
loomed over her.

But it wasn't his physical size and power alone that
made Willa's heart begin thudding with an unexpected
panic. It was the mysterious, new strength she sensed

thriving and building inside him. The strength that even when crippled and beaten had made it possible for him to survive through all he had. The same strength that now appeared as concentration and confidence in his eyes, and would soon become breathtaking demand *and* sensitivity in his touch. The strength that was evolving a violently angry, achingly brooding man into a devastatingly tender and generous lover, a caring man.

Suddenly Willa realized the magnitude of what she'd done. She was as responsible for creating this Zachary Denton as if she'd breathed the breath of life into him, as if she'd followed him to the edge of hell and fought Satan himself for his soul. Oh, yes, she knew why she was afraid.

No longer was this about sex and passion, nor did it bear even a faint similarity to any law of compassion she thought she'd ascribed to. It was about tomorrow, and all the tomorrows after that. It was about surrender and vulnerability. It was about dreams and fate…and destiny. Theirs.

She shut her eyes against the truth so poignant and clear, against the sharp pain that stabbed her heart. It was too much to hope that he missed it.

"What's wrong?"

She couldn't tell him.

To her amazement he murmured, "I understand," and stroked his cheek against her thigh.

The man was too much. Didn't he see? Already he was too much for her. "You tried to warn me. I thought I was listening."

"You're suddenly afraid of it all, the power of what's happening between us. The depth of it. Me."

She refused to cry because it wasn't fair to him, but she couldn't keep the fear out of her voice. "I don't want to fall in love with you,'' she whispered. ''I can't afford to feel that much again. I thought I was as strong as you. Stronger. I thought I could survive this. But you…this…it's devouring me.''

It was a terrible honesty. It would have hurt any weaker man. But to her amazement Zach simply raised himself above her and framed her face in his hands.

''You have to.''

''Zach…''

''You pulled me out of the darkness. Now I belong to you. And you belong to me.''

Just as if he'd chiseled the words on a stone tablet, he made them the truth with his kiss, absorbing her cry of protest and willing her to accept his heart in return. She couldn't have explained it any other way. And realizing she couldn't deny the truth, either, she wrapped her arms around him and clung fast.

This time he was the one to lead the way from darkness and terror, and the ride was breathtaking. An escape to freedom, she thought at one point as he moved down the bed again to finish undressing her.

She reveled in the clean freshness of the cool air buffeting her bared body. Then came a different pleasure as Zach began to cocoon her in his heat, inflaming her with his hands and mouth, until he had her writhing against the already twisted bedding, feverish in anticipation. The instant she felt his breath on her thigh, hers locked in her throat. Then as he whispered hoarse words of encouragement and adoration, he closed his mouth over her, and raced her to a release she thought impossible.

She hadn't begun to recover, wasn't sure she would ever regain control of her body again when he rolled onto his back and drew her over him. She thought she was exhausted, drained, and yet the moment she looked into his eyes, heard him whisper, "Willa," like a prayer, she knew she wanted him inside her as badly as he wanted to be there.

The sensations were strong, almost painful as she sheathed him. He felt it, too; she saw it in the veins swelling at his temples and along his neck. Then, his hold on her hips bruising, he showed her what he wanted.

The pace and energy turned her still-quaking body into a mass of excruciating need. With a sob aching in her throat, she gave him the wild ride that drove him deeper and deeper into her. At the very instant she knew she would tear apart, a hoarse cry ripped from him and she felt his pulsating release echo through her. Or was it hers again? Dazed and totally depleted, she slumped against him. And long after he wrapped his arms tightly around her, his body continued to spasm in hers, hers around his.

It didn't surprise Zach that they slept. They'd needed the emotional break as much as the physical one. But what did come as a stunning revelation as he opened his eyes and read the illuminated numbers on the night-table clock, was the hour.

"Past nine o'clock. Do you believe it?"

He stretched and turned on the light to consider Willa. She still lay on top of him and even tousled and squinting, looked heartbreakingly lovely to him.

"I believe it. It was the comfortable blanket I had," he teased, running a finger down her model-straight nose. But remembering the relentless and compelling urgency with which he'd driven them both, he sobered.

"You okay, sweetheart?" He loved how tenderness made her eyes shimmer.

"Mmm. Despite my shaky start, I think I'll make it. But," she added, sitting up, "only if I find something to eat. I'm starving."

With a speed and energy that exhausted him all over again, as well as pinched his ego, she began stretching, and then rummaged through the sheets for her things. Greedy, he caught her wrist and tugged her back down.

"Where's the fire, fair maiden?"

She laughed softly. "It's been over twelve hours since we ate. Aren't you hungry?"

"I'm not sure. Looking at you makes me forget."

The smile died and Willa hid her face in the mat of hair covering his chest. "Zach…you can say the most beautiful things. What you said to Detective Pruitt about me…? I cherish that, too."

"You make them easy to say." He stroked her cheek as she sat up again, but the reminder of Pruitt cast an unignorable shadow over the joy they'd been discovering with each other.

Why hadn't they heard from the cop?

Studying him, Willa asked, "Did I actually hear Detective Pruitt tell us that he was going to talk to Judith tonight?"

"He damn well should," Zach muttered, scowling. "We've done everything but hand her to him on a platter."

"I wish he would call." She gave him a sympathetic look. "You haven't made much progress writing today, have you?"

She couldn't know what an understatement she'd made. But rather than admit that, he sat up to press a kiss to her forehead. "You think I'm going to complain about that after what we shared?"

Knowing if she continued to look at him like that, he was going to keep her in bed for the rest of the night, he sighed. "Maybe you'd better see if there's anything edible in either of the refrigerators."

"I know we have eggs and bacon left from what I brought over this morning," she told him, slipping off the bed and heading for the bathroom. "So we can always have another omelet. Oh, blast." She whirled around. "Zach, can I borrow a shirt until morning?"

Her naturalness and beauty made his mouth go dry. "Nope," he barely managed, and had to swallow. "In fact, I think you should come back to bed."

Murmuring her thoughts about insatiable men, she went to his walk-in closet and came out barely wearing a blue dress shirt. It, like the suits it matched, hadn't been touched in ages. The thing definitely looked better on her.

"Okay," he said, changing his mind, "you can borrow that one—under the condition you don't button it."

She flicked the tails at him as she disappeared into the bathroom, and Zach slumped back against the pillows feeling much the same heady emotions he had when he'd downed his first beer. Only with Willa's help, the high could last a whole bunch longer.

Sweet heaven, I could get used to this.

The phone rang, wiping off the dreamy grin he knew was on his face, and he reached for the cordless unit beside him.

It was Pruitt. And the detective wasted no time in getting to the point. "You two okay over there?"

"Yes. Why?"

"Your ex-wife is dead...and both Sachs and Elias are nowhere to be found."

CHAPTER TWENTY-TWO

She'd heard the phone, but fought the urge to dash out and find out who was calling. Besides, she knew...and suddenly she wasn't sure she wanted to know what he had to say.

Instead, she took her time freshening up. Zach needed the privacy, she told herself.

But minutes later, as she faced herself in the mirror and buttoned his shirt, she also had to face what she was doing. She hadn't rushed out because she wasn't ready to leave this oasis she and Zach had found for a few blissful hours.

Something had happened. She could feel that, too. Would it end everything?

As soon as she opened the door and saw him sitting on the edge of the bed with the phone in his hands, the fear vanished. She rushed to him and sank to the carpet between his knees. "What?" she whispered, taking the handset from him. She placed it on the table without taking her eyes off his dazed face. "What's happened?"

"Judith is dead. He strangled her."

Willa gripped his hands, but she didn't make any empty expressions of sympathy. They both knew that unlike the people Judith had hurt, she'd deserved her fate. On behalf of the innocent, Willa asked, "Which one?"

"They don't know yet. They can't locate either Elias or Sacks."

Why couldn't they? This was Vilary, for pity's sake,

not New York City! She didn't resist when Zach drew her into his arms. Whether he was offering his strength or asking for her comfort, it felt good. "They'll find him," she said for both of their benefits.

"Yeah. But will it be soon enough?"

They couldn't afford to think like that. She struggled to focus on what could be explained. "When did they find Judith?"

"Only a short time ago. An observant neighbor saw smoke coming from the house and called it in, even though the person saw Judith's car in the driveway. The body had been dragged into the kitchen in the hopes of making it look like she'd been trying to put out an accidental stove fire. Hell, all they would have to have done is check the refrigerator to know that was a joke. She was the one person who cooked less than I do. Was. Did you hear how easily I can talk about her in the past tense?"

Willa winced at the raw edge in his voice and hugged him tighter.

"As soon as he can cut someone loose from there, Pruitt's going to put a patrol car out front," he murmured, resting his cheek on the top of her head.

"Do you really think that's necessary? Surely whichever of them killed Judith, he's long gone by now."

"Let's hope so. But I'd rather the cops play it safe, especially where you're concerned."

"Wait a minute." Willa saw a flash through the sheers. She eased out of Zach's arms and went to the window. "I think that's the patrol car now. He must have his lights— Zach! My house is burning!"

She couldn't believe it. It had to have started minutes ago, perhaps as Zach spoke on the phone, because the flames were already spreading in both her bedroom and the kitchen. Horrified, Willa ran for the door. "Call 9-1-1!"

"Where do you think you're going?" Zach yelled at her, telephone in hand. He grabbed for her, but missed, tumbling off the bed and hitting the floor with a loud thud. "Willa!"

She was already in the hall. "It's my *house,* Zach! I know what to do," she added, bumping into the door frame of his office. "I'll take your gun. Make the call!"

She sped across the room, grateful for the computer screen's light and jerked open the top drawer. Grabbing the revolver, she saw the remote control for the front door and grabbed it, too.

Zach had managed to make it to the hall when she ran out and she barely escaped another desperate grab.

"Willa—for the love of heaven…!"

"Call!"

She felt his fury and frustration and her heart went out to him, but he hadn't seen the fire. She couldn't just stand and watch. And it wasn't stupid vanity about all her hard work, either. It wasn't the money. She had insurance.

How could she put into words that it was the assault, the rape of her memories?

So she ran through the dark house with him screaming and cursing behind her. If she could get the garden hose started, she might be able to contain the damage. And with every step she prayed, *Forgive me, Zach. But he's not destroying another life.*

In the foyer she grabbed her keys lying beside her purse on the entryway table and punched the remote. The door creaked open, letting in a gust of hot, humid air.

Wind! If the fire department didn't get here soon, the

fire would take more than her house. *"Hurry!"* she screamed up to Zach, and thrust open the screen door.

She ran as fast as her bare feet allowed, hating that the soles were so tender, and hoping she wouldn't lacerate them and slow herself down. The fire downstairs had already reached the dining room. The oak table, the second piece of furniture she'd chosen with A.J. after their bed, was beginning to scorch.

At the front door she came up against another hurdle. For whatever reason the timer hadn't gone off and, except for the eerie glow beginning to flicker through the sheer draperies, it was impossibly dark.

Once she had it unlocked, she felt the door for heat as she'd learned during safety courses at the mall. It wasn't hot, so she felt fairly confident in thrusting the door wide.

No blast of flames assaulted her, but the smoke was getting thick, rolling down from the ceiling like some malevolent creature from one of Zach's darkest nightmares. She ducked to peer beneath the thick, pungent mass, but she didn't see or hear any sign that someone was in there. That didn't mean he wasn't, though.

The doubt finally hit her. Her own mortality. And the ugliness swelled until everything seemed to be mocking her, the smoke alarms, the ravenous flames...

She didn't know what drew her gaze to her wedding photo, to A.J., but she stared at that wonderful thumbs-up, piece-of-cake smile, and not since the night she'd lost him had he felt closer.

Something calmed within her. She took a deep breath and reached into the flower bed to tug the hose carriage onto the front stoop. Then grabbing the nozzle, she turned on the water pressure full force and ducked inside.

Once through the doorway the temperature shot up at least thirty degrees, the noise became deafening. But the worst of it was that after only seconds of spraying into the dining room, she knew she didn't have a prayer. A window exploded upstairs. Another went in the kitchen. With the breeze seeping into the house, she knew her only hope now was the fire department.

But she wasn't ready to leave yet. Although the smoke was already reaching the floor and her eyes were beginning to tear up and burn, she crab-walked toward her photograph. It was as she reached up that she heard the slam.

The force shut off the water, and she knew no wind was strong enough to have done that. Horrified, coughing and wheezing, she dropped the hose and dashed for the door. She pulled, jerked and beat at it. Not even the knob budged.

"Open up! Help! Let me out!"

Her cries only made the coughing worse. Oh, God, she thought, the smoke. Thinking became a struggle, but breathing was already an impossibility.

He couldn't have locked her in, she told herself gripping the keys so tight, they cut into her left palm. She could get out...if she used the gun. The gun.

She tightened the fingers of her right hand around the revolver, stepped back from the door, aimed and fired. Then she fired again. And then again.

The third shot won her a scream. She grabbed the doorknob and jerked, and even though she couldn't see a thing for the smoke and the tears, she burst from the house, holding the gun before her.

She stumbled as if she were drugged or drunk or both. The fresh night air felt wonderful wafting against

her burning skin, but she sobbed at the agony it caused
her lungs. And her eyes...

She practically stumbled over him. He lay facedown
and she couldn't tell where she'd hit him, but the blond
hair and his muscular build told her who he was.

"Ger?" she wheezed. "How badly are you...hurt?"

She couldn't say anything for another minute. A new
rage of coughs nearly brought her to her knees.

Finally, convinced he was either out cold or dead,
she glanced back toward Zach's in time to see him
crawling out his door. She rose and waved. Tried to let
him know she was all right, but coughed and gagged
instead.

"Willa—no! Behind—"

The blow caught her in the small of her back knocking the wind from her lungs. She had a momentary flash
of the ground racing up at her, the gun and her keys
leaving her hands, and then her head exploded into mil-
lions of lights, each tiny dot erupting into a pain as
horrific as anything she could have imagined.

She couldn't see, couldn't catch her breath. Then she
felt his hands closing around her throat and she knew
she wouldn't again. Ever.

Her mind said to fight, to claw and kick. To *live*. But
her body refused. She had nothing left.

I'm dying, Zach! Oh, Zach, I'm...

Blissfully, the agony began to grow vague, her panic
waned to a sorrow. And then there was only the welcome darkness.

"No!" Zach clutched at the screen door as a dull
knife ripped out his heart. *"No!"*

How could he have made it this far only to fail?
Willa! Sweet Jesus, please...

"Here I am, you son of a bitch!" he screamed at Ger, pain and rage giving him a new strength. "It's me you want. Come and get me!"

Dazed, and bleeding from his side, Ger rose from Willa and started toward him.

So this was it. Zach wiped ruthlessly at the tears flooding his eyes and, empty except for grief and hatred, he started crawling back to the elevator. He knew what he had to do. Gerald Sacks wasn't going to go through any trial and be found guilty by reason of insanity. He was going to hell. Tonight.

And I'm going to take you there.

He crawled like the reptiles he used to watch race across the desert sand. "Come on!" he taunted over his shoulder. "This is what you want, isn't it?"

The wounded, winded man appeared in the doorway just as Zach reached the elevator and slammed the cage shut.

"Stop, Zach. It doesn't have to be like this."

"Bull. Come on, you coward!" He pressed the button and the car rumbled into action.

Ger stumbled to the stairs and began climbing like a robot. He was halfway up when Zach reached the second floor and threw open the gate. With his legs and back killing him from the exertion, Zach mostly dragged himself, but determined, he made his way toward his bedroom. It had the nearest dormer window.

As he passed Willa's clothes and shoes, he suffered another sharp spasm of grief. Tears threatened to blind him, but he used the rage to rip at the draperies and hoist himself up on the ledge. Then he released the lock and pushed up the window.

Sirens greeted him along with flashing lights, police cars and fire trucks. He saw men running. One raced for Willa. His darling. His love. He'd never said the words to her. The bastard had even deprived them of that.

Hearing Ger right behind him, he crawled, indifferent to his nakedness, out the window. Ger grabbed at his arm, but Zach beat him off.

"Come on," he growled, hatred seething in him. "Come on out here and get me."

"It's not my fault, Zach. It was never my fault."

"Yeah? Who's then?"

"Judy. No, I mean Judith." He rubbed his forehead. "I have to stop their voices. Too many… Tell them to turn off those sirens, Zach. I can't think." He shook his head. "Judy was the one who kept saying we weren't really related, that we could be together. But I knew it was wrong…and she—she was bad to me. She wouldn't leave me alone. I had to make her shut up. Why didn't she just shut up?"

What the hell? Zach couldn't begin to make sense out of the crazed gibberish, but he was determined to try and use it.

"Maybe she couldn't because she *was* right about you," he shouted at him. "And you know what? See all those people? They're wondering about you, too. And I'm going to tell them."

"No! Judith was right—you were never my friend! You were using me, too!" Furious, Ger climbed onto the roof after him.

Men yelled at them from below. Zach recognized Pruitt as he inched down the still-warm, composite shingles. The sharp flats bit into and scratched at his flesh, but he wanted to reach the gutter in case Ger tried to knock him over and he didn't get a good enough grip to take him with him.

The cop yelled something again, but he couldn't understand with all the noise. Besides, he no longer cared.

"Denton! I said, don't be a fool. She's alive! *Hold on!*"

Alive? He looked toward Willa again and saw two paramedics now had her sitting up and were holding an oxygen mask to her face.

"Willa…?" Joy replaced disbelief, as he saw her push the mask away, point toward him and try to break free from her two guardians.

Almost too late he sensed the movement beside him. He stiffened, but couldn't stop the brutal kick he took to the shoulder.

It sent him rolling like a fallen log down a mountain. But fortunately, he was close enough to the gutter not to build up too much momentum. He grabbed and stopped himself. Barely.

"Go down, Zach," Ger muttered, inching toward him, his expression mad, determined. With every few inches of progress, he reached with his heavy-soled athletic shoes in an attempt to land another kick. "Go down."

Zach swore silently. The guy sounded like a petulant child for crying out loud.

He looked over the edge of the gutter to consider his chances, trying not to think how moments ago it hadn't mattered. It would be a twenty-foot drop if he landed on the overgrown shrubs. If he missed, at least twenty-five or six.

He glanced back toward Ger and saw the younger man ready himself.

Pruitt yelled, "Don't do it, Sacks!"

Ger ignored him.

A shot rang out.

The bullet jerked Ger as it struck him in the middle of his chest. Almost immediately a circle of red began spreading toward the matching stain near his waist. For a moment he looked directly at Zach. Then, smiling, he lurched forward and tumbled down and over the roof, taking Zach with him.

CHAPTER TWENTY-THREE

"Look at you two. How the heck they agreed to release you from the hospital after less than twenty-four hours, I'll never know."

Willa exchanged smiles with Zach. After using the remote to release the front door latch for Detective Pruitt, she'd returned to Zach's bed and now snuggled happily beside him. Her attire was another of his shirts because her house had been deemed a total loss and she hadn't yet let busy Starla bring anything from the shop. She wasn't surprised when he snatched up his bathrobe from the foot of the bed and spread it over her bare legs—as well as he could with his left arm in a cast.

"They were glad to be rid of us," he told their visitor. "Refusing to stay out of her room helped."

Out of her bed, Willa amended silently. But it was true. As soon as he'd been checked out, stitched up and his broken arm put in a cast, he'd demanded entrance to her room and had used his now-famous glare on anyone who'd attempted to separate them. Although she'd tried to argue otherwise—mostly by hand signals and notes—he'd seen her injuries as far more severe than his, and he refused to let her out of his sight.

They were lucky. Fate had been generous to them. The doctors said she hadn't suffered any permanent damage to her throat or lungs, and that the hoarseness would eventually disappear, as would the bruises on her neck.

But most gratifying of all, Zach hadn't suffered any

new damage to his spine. The stitches at his temple would be out in about ten days, and he'd already proved the cast wouldn't keep him from showing her at every opportunity how much he loved her.

"Well, you'll be happy to know most of the press have resigned themselves to the idea that you aren't going to make a statement," Detective Pruitt continued. "They're packing up and pulling out. Moving like turtles, but moving."

"Good," Zach muttered, taking hold of her hand again. "And did you contact Willa's family?"

The older man's smile grew warmer as he focused on her. "Yes, I have. They were, admittedly, shocked and upset, but they're okay now. They understand you can't talk for a few days, and your parents are insisting on cutting their vacation short and returning to the States, but everyone sends you their love. If I were you, I'd expect some strong pressure about taking you back to Dallas for a while."

Willa shook her head adamantly, and inched closer to Zach. Although she took reassurance from the gentle squeeze of his hand, she knew he and her family would need time to get used to each other.

"All right, enough pleasantries. What the hell was this whole mess about?" Zach demanded, exposing his lack of patience with small talk, and with what had almost cost them everything.

If Detective Pruitt was offended, he hid it well. "Well, to start with, you heard Sacks correctly when you said he called Judith Judy because it turns out there were in fact *two* of them. The one he referred to as Judy was an adopted sister he grew up with in California. She was two years his senior. Not exactly a little angel. Neighbors who remember the family didn't recall when

or how the Sacks got her, but just about all said she
was a wild one. Er, promiscuous. It's believed she tor-
mented the boy badly, which explains where his problems both with his morality and his sexuality set in.''

"How'd you find all that out?" Zach asked, not doing a good job at hiding his curiosity.

"Professional secret," the policeman replied, recip-
rocating nicely. "You think I want to read about this in
your next book? In any case, somehow *your* Judith—"

Zach stiffened. "Never call her that again."

"Zach," Willa whispered as best she could, touching
his cheek. "He's only trying to explain."

He blinked, and then gave her an apologetic, haunted
look.

"Ms. Denton," Detective Pruitt continued, almost
kindly, "began receiving threatening notes, too. We lo-
cated quite a collection during our search of her house.
Being far more social and mobile than you, she had less
difficulty determining who her pen pal was—no doubt.
She started from the suspicion it was you or someone
you'd hired to either intimidate or harm her after your
unpleasant divorce.

"She was acquainted with Sacks through the health
club. And again, we can only speculate how she picked
up on the tidbit about Sack's sister. My guess is that
she wasn't all that different in her technique than Judy
and she apparently knew how to shrewdly manipulate
him, didn't she? Just as she must have used the fact that
Sacks had access to your house. She was one tough and
sharp cookie. Poor Sacks. He never stood a chance. He
went from idolizing you, Denton, and despising her, to
hating you, and worshiping her. We've been through
his apartment—it's all there the pictures on the walls,
the graffiti, sex toys, cut-up magazines and a few things

you're better off not knowing about. The head doctors and think-tank people who'll end up studying his case for suspect profiles are going to have a field day sorting through his psychoses. Maybe one day they'll be able to tell us what made him ultimately turn on Ms. Denton and slip completely out of control. Hopefully the transcript of your last conversation with him will help,'' Pruitt told Zach.

Zach thought it a miracle Ger hadn't turned on Judith sooner. ''What happened to the stepsister?'' he asked the cop.

The detective hesitated, then gave Willa an apologetic look. ''A more successful version of the punishment he inflicted on Ms. Denton. He raped then strangled her, and burned down the boarding house where she'd been living. The authorities were glad to solve the case. Ten years that one stayed open.''

If only things could have been resolved sooner, Willa thought, aching for Linden Leahy's family.

''Any change in the Porter woman?'' Zach asked, as if he'd been having similar thoughts.

Pruitt shook his head. ''But I do have some notes on Roger Elias. He sends his best wishes, by the way, but he's still a bit rattled that you'd had doubts about him.'' The detective scratched the tip of his nose and referred to his notes. ''Oh, it seems that bruise on his cheek was self-inflicted after an altercation with a young woman he'd picked up at a bar. He apparently misread her signals, and decided he'd rather have people think he'd been clumsy rather than, er, struck out.''

Zach rolled his eyes. ''Isn't there anyone out there who isn't having problems with their love life?''

Willa intercepted Detective Pruitt's wry look and smiled.

"As for Fraser," the policeman concluded, slipping his notebook back into his jacket, "it's my understanding that he's wiring certain funds to your bank today. I, of course, don't know what any of that means, but told him I was happy to pass on the message. By the way, he speaks of you with nothing short of reverence."

"Only because I'm not sending his butt to jail," Zach countered with more than a little bitterness.

"It's all turned out." Willa had heard him speak of Felix Fraser several times in the past twenty-four hours, and knew his sensitivity over the man's actions would linger for some time. "We can afford to be generous."

"Well, that's all I have to add. Anything more I can do for you folks?" the detective asked, beaming.

"Yes, ticket the laggers on your way out," Zach replied, looking for all the world as if he were serious.

Shaking her head, Willa thanked the man for all his help and escorted him out.

When she returned, she wasn't surprised to find someone entirely different waiting for her. Zach's strong, bold features had softened, the shadows were gone from his eyes, and when she accepted the hand he extended in invitation, his care in tucking her close to his side made her feel like the most cherished being on earth.

"What am I going to do with you?" she whispered hoarsely, tapping him on the chin. "How can you be such a sweetheart with me, and such a terrorist with nearly everyone else?"

"I'm not in love with everyone else. With *anyone* else. I love you." He took her hand again and pressed a kiss into her palm. "Tell me you'll marry me and you can spend the rest of our lives trying to reform me."

This wasn't a new proposal. He'd been attempting

variations on the same theme since their trip to the hospital in the ambulance. And she'd loved hearing them all. But she hadn't given him an answer yet, and was aware of the tension building in him.

"I know you love me," he said, his intense eyes searching hers.

"With all my heart. More than I thought it possible to love again." That was true, too. Last night when she'd felt A.J. so close, it was as if he had been watching over her, trying to reassure her, until she and Zach had been reunited in the ambulance. Then his presence had drifted away like candle smoke. It had been so sweet, and a little sad.

"Then what's holding you back? Is it the fact that we've known each other for only twenty minutes?"

Once again she shook her head, but she could smile this time, loving the humor that was beginning to creep out of him at odd moments. "That I'll leave for my family to fuss over."

"Then what?"

She sighed. "I just wanted to give you time to be out from under the pain medication and be thinking clearly. I wanted you to be able to change your mind if necessary, and be certain that it's not a case of pity that's making you say this because I've lost my house and every remembrance of my life before meeting you." Although the pain was building in her throat, she had to get all the words out. "I want you to be sure that I'm not going to be another of your projects."

"Projects?"

"Yes. An obsession you tackle in a book the way you deal with your fears one by one. I don't want you to wake up one morning and...be over me."

He shook his head, his gaze sweeping over every inch

of her face. "I can't believe you think that's possible. Let my beautiful queen go? My brave, stubborn lady who tried to protect her broken, haunted king, a king who tends to see dragons and conspiracies around every corner?"

"I'm not a marble statue on a board, Zach. I'm just a woman dealing with her own losses and fears, and trying to regain some faith in building again...dreaming again."

She watched as his gaze shifted to her throat, saw his eyes darken as he viewed again the ugly bruises, felt his fingers tremble against her, and his eyes amazingly brighten with the moisture she'd seen several times in the past twenty-four hours.

"You're my sanity, Willa. My beacon in the darkness. I know I can't offer you a conventional marriage with a husband who works nine-to-five, mows the lawn on Saturdays, takes the kids on camping trips and teaches them to swim in the local swimming hole."

"The last thing I want is for you to be someone you can't be or don't want to be," Willa rasped, dismayed that he thought she could want a stereotype—worse, a robot.

"Then love me, stay with me," he choked out, lowering his cheek to hers. He whispered urgently into her ear, "Say you'll be my wife, my lover and friend. My partner. Help me get through the nights when the shadows lurk too close. Lead me out into the sun and let me watch your smiles and laughter. Say it and spend the rest of our lives watching me thank the day you stormed my castle. Be *my* dream."

Why had she doubted he'd meant it? Because she'd believed as the novels warned, that "human beings never enjoyed true happiness in this world"? Well, none of those authors had ever seen the way love was radiating in Zachary Denton's eyes.

"Be mine," she whispered, drawing his mouth down to hers.

And oblivious to the injuries and close calls they'd experienced on their journey here, they clung to each other and eagerly sought the magic and ecstasy that Willa realized would be uniquely theirs.

* * * * *

Silhouette

SPECIAL EDITION™
Emotional, compelling stories that capture the intensity of living, loving and creating a family in today's world.

Silhouette®

Desire.
A highly passionate, emotionally powerful and always provocative read.

Silhouette®
Where love comes alive™

Silhouette

INTIMATE MOMENTS™
A roller-coaster read that delivers romantic thrills in a world of suspense, adventure and more.

SILHOUETTE *Romance*
From first love to forever, these love stories are for today's woman with traditional values.

SILGENINT

Where love comes alive™

From first love to forever, these love stories are
for today's woman with traditional values.

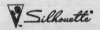 *Desire*

A highly passionate, emotionally powerful
and always provocative read.

V Silhouette®

SPECIAL EDITION™

Emotional, compelling stories that capture the
intensity of living, loving and creating a family in
today's world.

V Silhouette®

INTIMATE MOMENTS™

A roller-coaster read that delivers romantic thrills
in a world of suspense, adventure and more.